# Duchess and Dagger

## Crime Thriller

## Preetaa Bavaani

INDIA • SINGAPORE • MALAYSIA

ISBN 979-8-89744-457-1

Dedicated to my amazing parents

# Contents

# Acknowledgement

I would like to thank my grandparents for love and constant encouragement

# Chapter 01

## The Fatal Sip

As soft snowflakes drifted down, it felt like frost was hidden under a sheet of coldness. The sky seemed to be shivering as if something would shift in seconds. The clouds stormed over Heirshenfernern Palace which stood majestic in the south west of London City. This palace belonged to the Royal kingdom of Heirshen, an island in Northen Atlantic region. Royals of Heirshen continued to live in this Heirshenfernern palace for a century now after their kingdom were overthrown by democrats. They moved into London, building the palace of Heirshenfernern. The striking Royal palace's monolithic windows outline the appearance of winter. Behind these windows lies a world shown in photographs.

Inside the world was aglow with delicate details and refreshing settlements, the vision that could be seen the palace with high vaulted ceilings and sweeping arches seemed to breathe with an air of privilege, comfort, and power. This was a place in which time itself was frozen, only, somewhere within that stillness, an unseen shadow lay, lurking in the quiet of it, seen by none other than the perceptive eye.

The elegant cherry-red ribbons enveloped the ceiling and curled. this, rich crimson velvet draped along the walls and marble columns were seen.

Silver trays filled with petite sandwiches in the farthest corners, with crusts so carefully cut off they could be mistaken for miniature works of art. This delicate aroma of freshly baked pumpkin chiffon pie, cradle, flaky pastry through a rich cinnamon filling, mixes with the scent of freshly cut roses, their petals still dew-kissed from a garden long since closed off to the world. And on one of the grand tables that stretched across the ballroom like a river of decadent indulgence, there were mounds of clotted cream, scones rich with butter, and delicate, pale finger sandwiches stacked high with smoked salmon and cucumber. All of it sat within arm's reach, tantalizing the senses, inviting indulgence—and yet, beneath the soft glow of luxury, something darker stirred.

* * * * *

# Chapter 02

# The Calculated Detective

Ariana Caron stood at the threshold, her presence commanding, yet unseen by most of the guests. Tall, regal in a crimson coat that swirled around her figure like a cloak of authority, she cut through the sea of delicate silks and velvet with an elegance that made even the grand ballroom appear common place.

Unlike the other women in the room, draped in diamonds and pearls, Ariana's attire was plain—her dress simple but sharp, a deep black that clung to her form with understated grace, almost as though it had been painted on her. Her clothes stood out starkly against the swirling red and gold around her, a visual reminder of her solitude, of the distance she kept from the world she was constantly tasked with understanding and unraveling.

She had been invited to this royal gathering, yes, but she hadn't come for the food, the champagne, or the polished pleasantries. Her sharp mind made her one of the best-known detectives in country.

Elina's Eyes frequently shifted to her youngest brother, Julian, who was seated in a corner. Ariana observed the scene, paying attention to every detail. The way Lord Sinclair, with his noble behavior and silver beard, leaned over Elina, whispering something that resulted in her smiling. Eyes of Elina flashed once towards the very corner of the room, where her younger sister, Lavinia, remained. It was unnoticeable, but Ariana recognized that all these little things counted. Ariana's gaze returned to Elina, who was lifting her glass of champagne. She got into another hot debate regarding the Dor dynasty with Lord Sinclair. The discussion appeared to be continued with passion.

*  *  *  *  *

# Chapter 03

# The Great Shift

Something was going to shift.

And then it did.

It was then that high pitched cry, piercing scream was heard, its intensity was high. Its unexpectedness had paralyzed the group, transforming the polite smiles to confusion, then to terror. The voice belonged to Elina, but she was not speaking. She had collapsed over the table with a suddenness. Her champagne glass, half-filled, slipped from her grasp, and fell to the floor with a soft clink of porcelain meeting marble. The crowd pushed forward, some gasping, others in shocked silence, but Ariana was already moving, her boots clicking sharply against the marble as she weaved through the mass of people. Her eyes fixed on Elina's lifeless body.

* * * * *

# Chapter 04

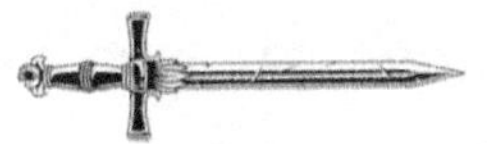

# Lifeless Body

She paused when she reached next to the historian. Her eyes dashed to the shattered champagne glass, then to the abandoned teacup within inches of Elina's fingers. The tea was warm when it was left behind. Now it was cold. A thin oily ring rimmed the edge of the porcelain cup. The scent was delicate, but Ariana knew it immediately, a bitter almond aroma. The distinctive scent of cyanide. The world around her was chaos. Some were screaming. Others grabbed their phones. Elina had been poisoned. That is, intentionally and exactly so. The whispers and the gossip filled the room. Ariana slowly rose from her seat, the pieces falling into place as she scanned through the sea of faces. Her eyes did briefly land on Julian again, his face so pale, eyes too wide. This was not just a killing. It was a message. As she turned, her heart crushed with thoughtfulness. It was merely the start. Her fingers wrapped around the lifeless form and willingly staining her hands with blood.

* * * * *

# Chapter 05

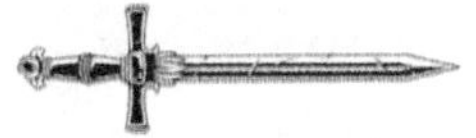

# **The Reluctant Promise**

Evening's sun glittered outside the palace and Ariana's eyes at last disengaged from the dead body of Elina Baxter. The once-shining ballroom now seemed far removed from the earlier grandeur, covered with an air of raw tension, the echoes of the chaos that had unfolded enduring in every corner.

Her keen eyes roamed the room. She observed the quiet faces, the tense murmurs, the tentative steps of the guests. Elina's death was a show, one that would have far reached effects in society like a stone cast into still water. To Ariana, however, this was not a show. This was business. It was something that must be resolved. Luna Baxter appeared beside her unexpectedly, her trembling hands betraying the calmness her words could not. "Ariana, please," she pleaded, her voice struggling.

"You must accept this case. Please. You're the only one that can possibly grasp it. You can determine who committed this."

Ariana stared at Luna; her gaze as cold as the marble floors beneath their feet. The younger sister's eyes were wide and desperate. Luna's body language grasping at the edge of her dress, the anxious glances around the room. This was not merely a sister's sorrow. No, it was a cry for justice. "Why me?" Ariana whispered. It required truth. Luna hesitated for an instant before she spoke. ""You have to take this case. Please. You're the only one who can grasp it. You can uncover who did this".".

"Because you are the only one who can read people, who can see beneath the surface. Everyone else is very close. They will not notice. They will not notice the truth.".

Ariana didn't even blink. She simply turned her back on Luna for a moment. She scanned the room once more, her keen eye moving from face to face. Ariana wasn't a thoughtless person. She faced Luna. "I'll take the case," she said bluntly. "But only because it's a mystery. And mysteries are what I'm best at." Luna nodded and said "Thank you. Thank you so much." Ariana said nothing. There was no need for words. There was only action now. And she didn't require anyone to remind her of that.

She hurried across the room and reached toward the grand double doors that led into the cool, fresh air of the evening. The door opened automatically as she approached. The chauffeur's pale face reflected in the window as he stood waiting for her to slide into the back seat.

All within the vehicle was an oasis of modernity. The interior stretched out in black leather seats. There was a combination of fresh polish fragrance and high-priced perfume. Ariana settled back; her thoughts already engaged. The car went along the London streets. She had taken a small leather case out of her bag and placed it on her lap.

The city was a blur outside the window, lights flashing by in lines of gold and silver. Ariana's thoughts were far from the world outside. She was determined. Elina Baxter's murder was just the start. There were threads hidden beneath. For Ariana, as the car slipped quietly through the darkness, mind turned to the next move. She required finding tales that others weren't talking. That involved going somewhere she could rely on to uncover the truth. A small newspaper shop. The faint meditative classical music demanded attention. Car stopped in front of a building. The faded sign hung outside, "Bramley's Papers & News,". Inside the shop we could see neatly stacked newspapers. She hurried to the door. The low overhead light was the only decoration in that shop. She recognized the smell at once, ink and aged paper. The shopkeeper, an old man wearing wire-framed glasses, looked up at her from the counter as she approached. He knew her on sight but said nothing. Ariana reached out and picked up a pile of papers, going through them with accuracy. She read over each headline until she came to what she was looking for. The report of Elina's death in evening news paper and the secret clues that were beneath the text. But one thing echoed. A passing mention of a certain connection. Subtle hints that lay beneath the surface. She purchased the papers without comment and exited the shop. The Rolls-Royce waited for her. She slid back inside and it drove off again through the dull London streets. She is headed towards her home. But there was one thing she knew with absolute certainty. This was only the start.

She would uncover the truth. Whatever it took.

*  *  *  *  *

# Chapter 06

# The Solitude of Silence

Ariana's gaze was fixed on the world outside, the diminished reflections of streetlights and distant traffic blurring into a seamless wash of neon colors. The city alive, chaotic, unyielding—felt distant. It was not her world tonight. Tonight, she would withdraw once again into the giant sanctuary, her home. The building was tall, a towering monument of smooth architectural delicacy. Glass and steel stacked like layers of ice. The view from the top floors alone could dominate the skyline, the city below sprawled out like a living map beneath her feet. Her heels clicked sharply against the wet pavement as she stepped out, her design framed by the soft light from the building's modern fixtures. The sound of rain softly pattering on the concrete was drowned out by the smooth sound of the elevator doors opening just for her. She was home. The space remained waiting for her return.

She took a moment, standing at the side of the private elevator, to admire the pure, minimalist design of the space. The high ceilings, the polished glass walls that allow light to pour in, the metallic fixtures and soft LED lighting—everything was artfully designed to create an atmosphere of absolute beauty. The doors of the elevator slid open. She entered and pushed the button for the top floor. As the elevator climbed, Ariana could glimpse the city skyline unfolding before her through the glass walls. London's lights shining in the distance could be seen amidst rainstorm. City noise was reduced to silence as she climbed above. She reached her penthouse. The whole floor was designed to her specifications. The floor-to-ceiling windows offered an uninterrupted scenic view of the city, the stormy night sky hanging like a blanket of shadows over the illuminated streets below. The penthouse was illuminated in soft, indirect lighting that poured from lower ceiling fixtures. The living room big enough to hold a mini conference, yet comfortable. It is made of polished concrete and hardwood floors. Furniture was placed around a fireplace. The walls of the living room were seen with modern pieces of art. Intellectual paintings were hanging. The vibration of the built-in sound system filled the silence with soft sound.

As she stepped further into the room a majestic piano was set against the opposite wall. But the fact that it was there, reminded her of the pieces of herself she forgot. Home was very clean. Open space. All the details, the lighting, the furniture, the art exactly resembled Ariana's thoughts.

It was silence and isolation which enabled her mind to travel back to the murder. The killing of Elina Baxter, the poisoned death, and the peculiar actions of the family that followed.

The study room which she now entered was silent with floor-to-ceiling bookshelves of books. Ancient tomes on history, philosophy, criminal psychology was there. Her case files were stacked neatly on her black-glass, polished desk. It was there, at that desk, that the change would start. The game would change.

The walls were lined with windows, but this evening the curtains were closed. The room was lit by designer lamps that emitted soft golden lights. A large cork board which occupied half of the wall was seen. Ariana placed photographs of the Baxter family. Elina, Luna, Isolde, Julian, covering the space, each image linked by precisely placed red thread.

Ariana stood there for a moment her eyes shifted between the pictures and the desk. Her fingers rested on the evidence of photographs spread out before her. The poisoned teacup, the champagne glass, and the excuses of the family, all the pieces of a puzzle. Her mind began to shift into gear, moving through the pieces with the precision of an experienced detective. She started constructing a case.

She spoke aloud. "It's here. I'll find you."

And she would. The pieces of the puzzle were scattered, but they would come together, as she had done these many times before.

* * * * *

# Chapter 07

# **A Morning Reflection**

Ariana's alarm screamed, waking her from a troubled sleep. She hadn't slept the previous night. Memories tortured her. She gasped and rubbed her temples. Ariana rose to feet. There was a storm within her brain. She readied herself for yet another day of investigation.

The kitchen, with its spotless countertops and stainless-steel appliances, greeted her like an old friend. She opened a cabinet, retrieving a small ceramic mug. Her coffee machine was a hi-tech machine, sleek and silent. She filled the filter with the finest ground coffee.

The machine came to life, and the wonderful smell of freshly brewed coffee filled the room. The initial sip was bitter but that is her preference. She is doing this as ritual every morning. The coffee is needed highly to focus her mind. With coffee in hand, Ariana looked out of the windows at the city below her. The skyline, still masked in the quiet of early morning filled with peace. But within, she was not at peace. Elina's death, Luna's suffering face, the open questions went inside her mind. Ariana took a deep breath. She had work to do. She went in to the study room where piles of research papers and files could be seen. The desk was pristine with few essential items, her laptop, a selection of pens, and a new pad of paper for taking notes were seen. Her mind had already started working, quietly making a list of the facts. She began with the fundamentals who was present at the palace on the night Elina died? What was the timeline exactly? Ariana pulled out Elina's case file from the desk drawer. The vision of Elina, her body drooping over at the royal tea party, appeared in her mind's eye. She went through victim's personal background. She went through the essentials. Elina's academic life, her publications, her past relationships, her family life. But it was the personal relationships that were of greatest interest to

Ariana. The rivalry with her younger sister Isolde is known but what about the others in her family? What about the others at work? Who might have had a motive to kill her?

Still keeping the file open, Ariana then wrote Elina's name in capital letters on a new A4 paper. Below it, she started making a list of questions. Questions that would help her in the investigation:

- Who was Elina closest to?
- How were her relationships with her family members?
- Was there any history of conflict with any specific persons?

Before she could go deeper, her phone ringed. It was Luna.

Ariana answered the call. "I'll be there soon," Luna said softly to which Ariana agreed. Ariana needed to concentrate. She had to be sharp minded. Her gaze shifted to the wall where a big corkboard was mounted, covered in pictures and bits of string. The early stages of a case were always messy. Thoughts and information, all scattered. But once she began, the connections would start to make themselves, as they always did. She would fit this puzzle together. She took out the pictures one by one and looked at the newspaper stack beside her. Old ink scent filled the room. She was ready. She cleaned the workspace, putting papers into bundles and filing the papers in front of her. This was how it always began. It was 8:30 a.m. and someone knocked at the door. Luna had arrived.

Time was now. Luna stepped into the penthouse. She was obviously nervous when she moved inside. But despite the nervousness, there was something infinitely thankful in her eyes when she looked at Ariana.

"I. I don't thank you enough," Luna said. "I need you to get to the bottom of who did this."

Ariana didn't say anything immediately. She merely nodded. Sitting down at the desk, she indicated the chair facing her. "Sit down, Luna. We have a great deal of work to do." Luna sat in the chair. Her eyes went to the corkboard. "Okay," Ariana started, her tone firm. "I'm going to go through all we know about Elina." She picked up the large pile of papers, pushing them in Luna's direction. She carefully unfolded each page. In A4 pages each one a different strand of Elina's life. Ariana's gaze rushed back and forth between the pages, reading the details.

She started to place them out individually, the first piece of the puzzle falling into place.

"I must know everything about her, Luna," Ariana went on. "Her life, her fears, the people she associated with, the enemies she had. Only then will we have chance of finding the killer."

Luna nodded. As Ariana began to read through the first file. They were about to reveal secrets. Secrets that would change everything.

* * * * *

# Chapter 08

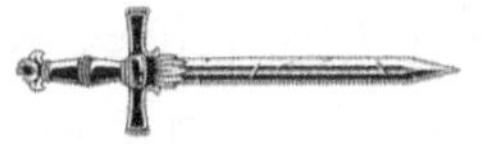

# A Web of Secrets Unraveled

The burden of the tragedy had fallen upon Luna that she couldn't remove. Luna's red eyes talked about the picture of a sister wet in sorrow. Ariana had no time for comfort. Taking a deep breath, she gave Luna a firm look.

"Luna," Ariana's voice came like thunder. "I want the most fundamental details of Elina's life. Everything. Full name, date of birth, schooling, career, honors, individuals she's collaborated with, co-workers, her friends. I'll require all of it." Luna nodded. She wiped a new tear away.

"Elina Sophie Baxter, Born on June 14th, 1985, London. The oldest of the Baxter children. She was always. different from the rest of us.

Dad was a historian, wrote about ancient civilizations, and Mom was a philanthropist who always part of charity events and parties, always in the limelight. Elina wasn't like them. She didn't like charity work.". She was only interested in her career. I suppose that's why we did not always get along.

Ariana jotted down the notes rapidly.

"Educationally, she graduated honors from Oxford University at 22. Studied medieval history particularly the rise and fall of royal families in Europe.". Then she became a professor at Oxford, soon becoming known for her pioneering work on royal dynasties. At 25, she was invited to Cambridge University as a full-time professor. That's when she actually began receiving awards. The Thirlwall Prize in 2017 was the pinnacle of her achievements. It was for her paper on 'The Political Conspiracy of Royal Dynasties,' which was ahead of its time.

"Awards, you tell me?" Ariana narrowed her eyebrow. "Go on."

Luna nodded. "Not only did she receive the Thirlwall Prize, she also received the highly respected Fulbright Fellowship for Research in 2015 that supported her research in Europe.". She was shortlisted for several academic awards and was a regular speaker at academic conferences in Europe and the US. She was absolutely private, you know. She didn't really have any close friends just professional contacts.

"Private. Ambitious" She put down a detail about her workplace behavior. "And what did she do about her personal life? Family members? Coworkers? Social circle?"

Luna's face nervous over again, but she pressed on "She was... difficult. Her relationship with Isolde and me was not easy.". Isolde was always the odd one out. Didn't care about the academic and not the one who considered awards or glory. Elina hated that. And then there was Lavinia, our other sister, she was reserved, always. Julian was too young to know any of this. He was close to Elina as she convinced everyone that the entire family would be ruined like isolde, lavinia and myself and kept teaching Julian her way of life. Elina admired Lord Sinclair who was her mentor at Oxford. Ariana's eyes narrowed. "Lord Sinclair. Tell me about him." Luna asked curiously "are you not close with him?". Ariana eyes sparkled as she calmly broke out, "yes, we are indeed close as my best friend Hannah is his niece but from Elina's life I wanted to know. Luna hesitated for a moment, but then spoke

"Lord Sinclair was Elina's tutor at oxford. He's an influential man, a big name in the academic community. Always supporting in the background when Elina was giving papers. He drenched her in compliments about her achievement. Elina was always suspicious of his intentions. She even told me once that she believed he was using her work to advance his own career."

Ariana jotted down his name on her suspects list. She then pushed a pile of papers to Luna. "I've compiled the main facts. Let's analyze this step by step." Ariana questioned Luna, "why do you suspect Sinclair so much"

Luna reacted swiftly "he was the last one to talk to her and I ju. Jus. tt heard he obtained 1 kg of cyanide"

Ariana continued calmly "yes indeed he obtained a full kg but you remember he is doing business in the mining and he designed weapons by hand using cyanide."

Ariana kept going "Elina consumed 3 drops of cyanide in her tea, you can't take decisions like this based on actions I think suspect may be in your family too"

Luna grabbed the documents from Ariana's hand asking "What do we do now?". Ariana replied "Now, we execute the plan. I'll be applying my 9 Key S Rule, step by step."

**Secure the Scene:**

"We'll need to ensure that all evidence is handled properly. I'll coordinate with the forensic team and make sure no evidence is disturbed." The ballroom is secured for our investigation

**Separate the Suspects:**

"We'll separate the suspects and gather statements. Everyone at the palace that night needs to be taken in for investigation. We'll start with Lord Sinclair and then your family."

**Scan the Scene:**

"We'll investigate Elina's study room and the rest of the house and see if there is anything that's out of place. Her study room is where she stored her research. There may be something that we have missed."

**See the Scene:**

"Who came and went through the palace? Where was everyone at the moment that Elina was killed?

**Sketch for Evidence:**

"We go to her study room, her bedroom, the dining room, and the areas where she used to spend the most time."

**Search for Evidence:**

We will thoroughly search Files, emails, research documents, anything that may provide a clue

**Secure and Collect Evidence:**

"We will collect the evidence Nothing should be missed."

**Scan and Examine the Evidence:**

"Forensic analysis. We'll have the toxins in her food and drink tested. Let's find out if there are traces of other poisons or chemicals."

**Scan the Bodies Postmortem:**

Full post mortem is being done to find out exact cause of death. Was she poisoned? Were there other signs of foul play?

"This is how we will go about it. One step at a time" Luna took in the plan and nodded slowly. "What happens to your Three Clauses plan? You mentioned that was crucial."

Ariana nodded. "Yes. The Three Clauses approach: Examination, Correlation, Interpretation."

**Examination:** "We will examine every single piece of evidence—every word, every document, every conversation. Nothing will be left to chance."

**Correlation:** "We'll correlate all the facts. Does Lord Sinclair is a prime suspect? What about the other suspects? "

**Translation:** "And then we'll interpret what we find. We will make the connection, and we will determine who is murderer."

* * * * *

# Chapter 09

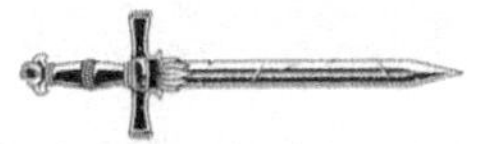

# The Perfect Team

Bell rang. "Albert, open the door," Ariana instructed. The door opened, and the first woman stepped in. Her presence was immediate—cool, controlled, and unshakable. Dark hair was pulled into a tight ponytail, her posture straight and strong, as if she carried the weight of countless situations like this one. She didn't need to say anything at first; her eyes did all the talking. Cold, focused, and calculating, she seemed to take in every inch of the room with a practiced glance, as if nothing could escape her notice.

A man followed closely behind, his tall frame almost blocking the doorway. He had an intensity about him—dark eyes that seemed to see everything. They flicked straight to the corkboard Ariana had already started filling with evidence. His gaze lingered on the photographs and notes, a quiet sense of authority about him as he took it all in, piecing together a puzzle no one else could yet see.

Next came the woman with restless energy, moving with purpose and barely contained excitement. Short, with platinum blonde hair that stood out in the dimly lit room, she had an air of impatience, her hands already twitching toward the papers on the desk, eager to dive in. There was something urgent in her every movement, as though she could hardly wait to get to the heart of the matter.

Behind her, a second woman entered, her gaze cool and piercing. Her brown hair framed her face, and her hazel eyes were sharp—calculating. When her eyes locked onto Ariana's, it wasn't just an exchange of looks; it felt like a silent joke, a brief but intense battle of trying not to laugh. She smiled heavily at her. There was something almost predatory about her, something that made the air feel a little colder.

Finally, the last man entered. Tall, composed, with an almost eerie calm about him. His dark eyes scanned the room, every detail absorbed in a way that suggested he missed nothing. There was no rush in his movements—he took his time, deliberate and careful. His gaze never wavered, and his steady presence seemed to hold the group together.

All of them were strong in different ways, in different methods of working, but together, they formed a team. Ariana stepped forward, her voice cutting through the thick tension in the room, "Luna, this is my team. Let me introduce you."

She gestured to the first woman, the one with chocolate brown hair. "This is Hannah Sinclair," Ariana said, her gaze flicking to the sharp-eyed woman, who gave a small nod, her stare never wavering. "She calls herself Hannah, but you'll find that she's not one to hide anything—especially when it comes to getting answers."

Next, the woman with platinum blonde hair, still buzzing with restless energy, stepped forward. "Seraphina Sunfield," she announced, her voice confident but edged with excitement.

She seemed almost eager to get to work, her eyes already scanning the room for clues.

The first tall man, standing still with quiet authority, gave a small smile and a slow nod. "Benedict Thornfield," he said, his deep voice calm, but it carried weight. Benedict was the kind of man whose presence grounded the room, the type who didn't rush to conclusions, but never missed a thing.

The second woman, the one with a tight ponytail called herself sharp-eyed and poised, stood next to Benedict. "Maya Wren," she said simply, her cold gaze taking in Luna, measuring her before even speaking. There was something about her quiet intensity that made it clear she was a force to be reckoned with.

Finally, the last man who was the bald one stepped forward. "Sebastian Crove," he introduced himself, his dark eyes locking onto Luna's with a calculating sharpness. His presence was solid, like a rock anchoring the rest, but there was a stillness to him that felt just as unnerving as the rest of the team. Each one of them had their own kind of strength, their own way of working, and together, they created a dynamic force that Ariana had clearly trusted to solve what was coming. Ariana stood and faced them all, her gaze cutting through the group.

"Okay, everyone. Time to get to work. We have a killer to catch. Let's begin with the investigation of Lord Sinclair. I want a complete report on his activities that night, and I want it by the end of today."

Then we proceed to Elina's family

Then other lesser-known rivals

Hannah remains with me we will fill up the corkboard and go through documents for information.

Seraphina get postmortem report as quick as possible. Benedict and Sebastian make investigations at the murder room

Maya follow up the suspects and request a chemist to test for toxins in the food, tea cup and champagne.

As the team went away, Ariana turned back to Luna,

"We'll find out what happened to Elina. I promise."

Luna nodded, trusting Ariana more and more and expected this would ultimately bring justice to her sister's premature demise.

*  *  *  *  *

# Chapter 10

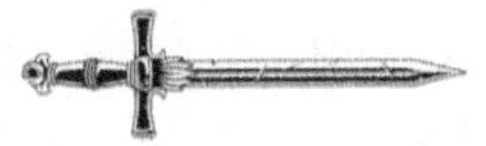

# The Corkboard

The golden cream curtains fluttered lightly in the breeze, their gentle movement like a soft whisper in a room heavy with tension. The sunlight streaming through them cast ethereal ripples across the floor, bathing everything in a surreal, almost haunting light. It was as if the room itself was trying to breathe, to release something that had been tightly held in for far too long.

Ariana's attention was momentarily caught by the mesmerizing dance of the light. But it didn't last. The sharp screech of her chair as she pushed herself back sliced through the stillness of the room. Her eyes, dark with intent, snapped back to focus. The hypnotic glow faded as she took control of the space around her, pulling the curtains closed with a swift flick of her wrist. The room darkened, as if retreating into a quiet, threatening cave, the harsh daylight outside now softened into an almost cruel calm.

She inhaled deeply, her chest rising with the weight of the task at hand. The tension in her shoulders was palpable, the tightness of her grip on the arms of her chair betraying the deep, gnawing anxiety that threatened to surface. Ariana's gaze met Luna's, a flicker of something sharp passing through her eyes. It was a look so cutting, so cold, that it seemed to slice through the air between them. Her voice came out in a tone that could freeze the very atmosphere in the room. Her words were like thousands of knives stabbing a person at once ruthless efficient clear

"Luna," she commanded, carving its way through the silence. "Take that stack of papers. Sort them into three distinct columns.

1. Elina's success.
2. Elina's personal life.
3. Elina's death."

Luna blinked, the sharpness in Ariana's voice throwing her momentarily off balance.

But her resolve quickly returned, and with a subtle nod, she moved to the stack of papers, each one like a tiny thread unraveling a much larger, much darker story. Ariana's words continued to slice through the stillness of the room, their weight settling on Luna's shoulders.

"Organize them according to the most significant aspects of her life. Theories about her death, her career achievements, her personal life Anything and everything. You know the drill. Use the color ribbons:

1.  red for death,
2.  blue for success,
3.  green for personal life."

Luna's hands trembled slightly as she reached for the papers, the weight of Ariana's unspoken expectations pressing down on her like an invisible force. Ariana's voice, now sharper still, held no room for mistakes.

"Mark each article from Bramley's Papers & News with the black marker. We cannot afford to miss any detail."

# Chapter 11

# The New Suspect

The giant black and red cabinet stood in room's corner, it has shiny and polished exterior. The dark black border contrasted with the fiery crimson highlights. It is secrets vault to Ariana. Rows of neatly arranged writing items took up the first row. Slim pens and markers in every color could be seen. The pens were separated by color, from pale pastel colors to dark, rich tones, each was kept for its own particular task. Red pens for essentials, black for accuracy. Markers, thick and thin.

Then came rows of journals and notebooks on the shelves. Some in leather covers, others plain. Behind them were glass containers full of bright tubes of paint. Reds, Blues, and Whites. Alongside them were brushes, their delicate bristles were sharp. The lower drawers held color coded boxes of thread silk, cotton, and linen; each spool marked with an alphanumeric code that only Ariana knew. At the back of the cabinet the locker was there which contained important documents, photos, and evidence pieces. Everything she required for her investigations. The lock was old fashioned but looked powerful. Ariana's eyes moved through the room. She lifted the lid on the box. She approached the deep blood red strand. "Shade 441," Hannah's commanding voice came. She moved forward and spoke. "We reserve that for dagger killings, not poisonings. Shade 345 is reserved for poisonings."

She thanked Hannah and gone for lighter red. The correction was effortless. She picked up a sheet of paper from the pile. Gently she stuck a small bit of pale-yellow tape to its corner. While doing this her eyes, focused entirely on her work, whispered "Elina Sophie Baxter" to the empty room, the words soft but with meaning.

Hannah, her face set in a mask of concentration, was absorbed in cutting out photographs from a massive, poster-sized photo collage that covered part of the table she was working on. The room's silence was broken when Ariana stood up from chair. "Albert," Ariana spoke in a sharp tone, "Get me some snacks."

In seconds, Albert arrived. He wore a neatly pressed black-and-white suit. The freshly baked croissant he offered Ariana was warm and flaky, its scent cutting through the tense air. Along with it, he presented a cup of coffee, cream swirled into the dark liquid like a shadow in the depths.

Ariana's drank coffee with deep thinking. "Morning, Madam," Albert spoke with concern. "Isn't this your coloring time?"

Ariana's lips got into a smile, her eyes never leaving work on desk, "Yes, Albert. But not in the middle of a case." The tone was sharp, but gentle. That is simply a fact. Albert did not answer at once, but his eyes stayed on her a fraction of a second. Then, with an afterthought, he said, "I got a message from your therapist. She says you have to do it three times a week."

Ariana's smile was ironic, brief. "Yes. I will. Thanks for the snacks."

Luna stacked the papers in three separate piles. Each of the stacks told Elina's disorganized existence her accomplishments, her secret life, and about her death.

"Luna", Are you finished? Ariana's voice came as thunder.

Luna set the stacks on the table. She was clearly breathless, but her voice seemed scared "I finished."

Ariana's gaze snapped to Luna, and in a steady voice she uttered,

"I think I discovered a new suspect for us where you have to assist"

Luna hesitated "Who is the suspect".

"Yes. They were born to the same family as Elina and she hated her. They were rivals, in a way. One wanted the center of attention, the other disliked it."

"Elina wouldn't have shared it with anyone." Luna added carefully

Ariana's voice was heavy. "Isolde, The middle child, She's too much of a rebel already. She is the perfect counterpart to do something extreme."

Luna, though, was disturbed. "Elina used to tell me that Isolde was. weak."

Ariana's pen started writing each word, each detail. "Continue," she forced, her voice low and alarming.

Luna's eyes went back and forth as she recounted the facts, each one leading up to something bigger. "There's footage filmed by Isolde herself. On it, she is vocally criticizing Elina, saying Elina's choices were 'dumb and wasteful." She had no respect at award events, always avoiding festivals when Elina was there. Except for the one where Elina was killed". Ariana's pen stopped halfway. Her eyes met Luna. "You don't have a detective's mind Luna, you said Isolde was rebellious, is she not the perfect fit to kill someone who she hates?"

Luna nodded, the seriousness of the statement felt uncontrollable.

Ariana's eyes were bright. "Brilliant, Luna. That's clear proof. From you I fitted the pieces together "

Before Luna could say a word, Hannah's voice came in. "I'll call Seraphina. She'll check on Isolde. I'll get a warrant in your name."

Every passing second bringing them nearer to an awakening they were not ready for. The thoughts were coming into position, but the image they created was too miserable. Luna's mind going wild, distractedly she drifted her hands to touch the golden leather bag that Elina had given to her. Gorgeous as it looked, now its touch evaluated as heavy as the burden of the fact that she had died. The printer gave out a "click" of its shot firing off, and complete, in the successful silence that descended. Time hung.

A knock at the door. A girl, no older than twenty, entered briskly, handing Ariana the printed sheet.

"The warrant should be with Seraphina by noon," Hannah's voice was cool, efficient. "We're moving forward."

As the girl departed. It was as if the very walls were closing on them, as the ticking of the clock brought them a little closer to the truth. And amidst the silence, one unquestionable truth shouted louder than all others. No one... no one was safe anymore.

* * * * *

# Chapter 12

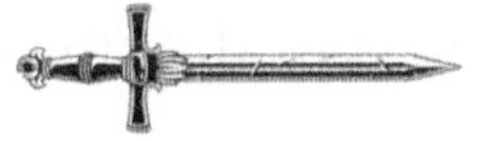

# The Blood-Stained Room

Ariana remained motionless. Her eyes fixed on the lush expanse of London beyond the window. The morning was peaceful. The sun shone in the pale blue sky, reflecting off the white, fluffy clouds that drifted by slowly. The savage storm was over, as if the universe itself was fed up in a breath. London had been torn by cold and incessant rain for what seemed like weeks, but today the air was perfect

A voice interrupted her train of thought, making her jump a little, but she felt like she couldn't let it show. "Madam, you were saying something about a celebration when the weather is good, and I could go home early," Albert said. Ariana never looked away from the view, her attitude clear. "Albert, yes. But not during an investigation. I'm certain Ella needs to learn how to behave in my house."

Albert nodded hastily, his steps thudding like a stampede on the marble floors, the sound of

A young woman appeared in the room seconds later.

Her voice was gentle, melodious, like the sound of a spring breeze through leaves. "My name is Ella Rhoades. I'm 23 and I will work well at any cost," she said, her eyes scanning Ariana's face for approval.

Ariana paused, her eyes carefully observed the girl. There was something about Ella something too suspicious, the flicker of her eyes and the nervousness in her face crowding her guilt, But Ariana kept that aside and concentrated on the rest instead. "Okay, Ella. If you're able to make things clean and tidy, you'll be good," she answered, her own voice calm and unyielding.

Ella nodded her head. Ariana's eyes moved back to the scattered papers on the table. Hannah had been searching through the piles of files when her phone beeped, its screen lighting with Benedict's name. She had ignored the initial call, but then it beeped again and this time picked up without comment. Hannah answered the phone on the second ring, her voice flat. "Hannah speaking. What is it?"

Benedict's voice crackled over the line, low and urgent. "Hannah, it's good. We finished the sample collecting. I need you to get to Palace." "I'll be there soon," she said, and hung up before Benedict could say anything else.

Ariana's mind started to spin. Elina Baxter killed in cold blood. The palace scene would be the same chaos it was. The investigation was just starting. And Ariana knew she had to be there before anyone else could step in. It was her case, her domain.

She looked at Luna, who was still in the corridor, waiting, anticipating the next step. "Luna, get into the car. We're going to the palace. We need to make inquiries into the room where Elina was killed."

Luna's face grew tight with fear, but there was no objection. Ariana went into her bedroom. The bed was clean, white sheets folded; pillows piled with neatness. There was a digital clock on the smooth mahogany side table, A moon lamp next to it, the closet door slid open easily, and inside was a wardrobe full of carefully selected pieces each outfit perfectly picked. Ariana selected a plain, but authoritative, black cropped top and denim jeans and a brown belt. Without delay, Luna trailed after Ariana down the corridor, her hands firm.

Ariana looked at her phone once more. Benedict had rung again twice. But she didn't call back. Her Rolls Royce was parked outside; the journey was rapid. By the time they arrived at Heirshenfernern Palace, the gates grew open slowly to the imposing mansion, and they stepped in into the sinister stillness within the palace.

The ballroom, once a testament to warmth and joy, now felt claustrophobic in its excess. Ariana's gaze cleared the room, her mind trying to connect the change in the character of the crime. The room still had a faintly bitter smell, "Two days ago,"

Ariana grumbled, looking over her shoulder at Luna, who had wandered over to examine the corners of the room. "A slow poison. Not an immediate thing. She had time to weaken. But this scene. It's a setup, Luna. Someone made it look like a murder of passion, a crime of violence." Luna returned with a gentle head shake. While Hannah added "There is no sign of struggle other than the initial poisoning". Ariana turned, eyes narrowed as she took in the area, remembering the possibilities. "A rapid acting poison, such as cyanide, is something that would produce instant symptoms. Had the poison been in the wine? Or had she taken it on something she'd eaten or drunk earlier in the night? Ariana's eyes narrowed. The wine, the positioning everything indicated an arrangement of events, intended to appear a brutal crime of passion. No, though, Elina's death was more deliberate, a stretching out of time. Whoever committed this murder must have known her intimately, knew her pattern, her trust. She stated to Hannah, "Inspect the wine glass. Don't touch it. I need to see if there is any residue at the end bits of something bitter, something out of the ordinary the cyanide is still there." Hannah nodded and stepped closer, studying the glass with a magnifying intensity. Ariana stood at the room's center, she could recall 2 days ago she cradled the lifeless body and smelled cyanide

Time was not on her side. The poison worked its way effectively but Ariana was sure. Elina's murder was not merely an act of hatred. It was something much more carefully planned. Someone within this very room, or someone who knew the victim closely enough, had planned her murder days in advance. Her thoughts flashed back to the possible suspects. Those who had been intimate with Elina. The ones who were privy to her, to her routines, to her timings. It was poisoning, sure. But it wasn't a simple poisoning. It was a message.

"Luna," Ariana's voice sliced through the still tension. "Scan the glasses for any trace of contamination, or anything that might have been used to dope her drink without her knowledge. We must locate the poison itself."

Ariana's heart rate increased, but she did not back down, knowing that the deeper aspect of the enigma was only beginning to surface. Two days had already passed, but the true investigation was just getting under way.

But the Duchess of Heirshen interruption reminded her that time was short. Duchess is a woman who married the duke (Prince of Heirshen). In European Royal families, Duchess title prevailed. The game had only just started. And Ariana wasn't going to let anyone hijack this investigation. She was in charge, and she would find out the truth, piece by piece.

Luna remained at her side, The Duchess of Heirshen walked in, her presence authoritative and uncompromising. Her elaborate dress rustled with every step; she broke the silence. Her pointed eyes immediately landed on

Ariana. Well, this is just ideal, isn't it?" she mocked, her tone soaking with sarcasm. "Another mess to be cleaned up. Elina never did learn how to stay out of trouble. She thought she could play the game and win. Weak. Ariana shifted her head, meeting the

Duchess's gaze. There was no question that her words were meant, intended to anger. And they succeeded, but Ariana was not shaken. Her eyes were cold, her face impassive. The Duchess moved closer to Luna, her mouth twisting into a cruel smile. "Poor Elina," she said, "Always the foolish one, too innocent for her own good. What a waste of life." Ariana's eyes contracted, her mouth compressing into a thin line. She was holding something back. Her words were an intentional insult, a move of power in a game Ariana had no plans on losing.

"Fine. Do as you please. But don't try to pretend you're in charge of this. This was all inevitable.".

And with that, Duchess departed the room. Ariana stood in silence, her thoughts racing in every direction. The investigation was only starting, and Ariana realized that this was but the beginning. There were secrets hidden here ugly ones and she was going to find them, cost be damned.

* * * * *

# Chapter 13

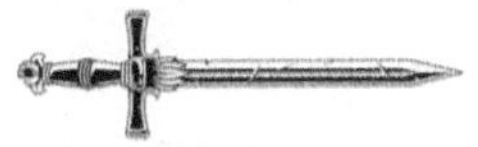

## The Sheets of Tracking

The sleek black Rolls-Royce continued its journey through the winding streets of London, the quiet hum of its engine providing a low, constant backdrop to the tension inside. Ariana leaned back against the seat, her fingers lightly tracing the edge of her phone, her thoughts swirling like the storm clouds on the horizon. The weight of Elina's murder was on her shoulders, pressing down on her in ways that words couldn't capture. It was as if the very air inside the car had thickened, each breathe a little harder to take.

The car slid past the grand facades of London's wealthiest neighborhoods, the towering mansions with their ornate iron gates and sprawling gardens. Ariana's mansion, a modern yet opulent reflection of her wealth and influence, loomed on the horizon—a sanctuary for her chaotic mind. It stood at the top of a hill, its sleek glass and stone exterior casting long shadows in the late afternoon light. Inside, everything was pristine, every corner of her home an embodiment of order and control.

She walked in, her sharp footsteps echoing through the marble halls. The air inside was cool, crisp, the faint scent of lavender and bergamot mingling with the sharp scent of freshly cut flowers. It was all so carefully curated—perfect in every detail. It was here, in the calm of her home, that Ariana felt the weight of her responsibilities most acutely. She closed the door behind her, exhaling slowly. For a moment, she allowed herself the luxury of quiet. The elevator doors slid shut with a soft *ding*, and the deep, humming sound of the elevator was the only thing breaking the silence as Ariana ascended to the top floor of her home. The polished silver doors gleamed under the soft lighting, reflecting her sharp, determined expression. Ariana rarely allowed herself time to pause, but right now, in this moment of transition, she did just that. The silence of the elevator, the plush carpet beneath her feet, the soft fragrance of sandalwood and vanilla filling the air—everything about this moment spoke of order, control, and immaculate precision.

The elevator hummed to a stop, the doors sliding open with a quiet *shush* as she stepped out onto the upper floor. The lights automatically flickered on, casting a warm, golden glow across the expansive space. It was as if the entire top floor was designed to breathe calm into her frayed nerves, but Ariana knew that even the quietest corners of her sanctuary couldn't hold back the storm of thoughts brewing within her. She was too far gone into this investigation, too immersed in the darkness of it all.

*  *  *  *  *

# Chapter 14

# The Comfort of Home

The bright, airy atmosphere of her home—a perfect mirror of her perfectly controlled life—couldn't erase the weight of the truth that loomed just beyond reach.

Her home was an embodiment of herself—sharp, sleek, and efficient, every element designed to evoke a sense of sophistication, power, and isolation. The floors were gleaming marble, a creamy white that caught the golden light and shimmered like water under the sun. The walls were a soft dove gray, adorned with minimalist abstract art that gave the space an almost clinical precision. Everything was arranged with meticulous care, every book, every piece of furniture in its exact place. There was no clutter, no excess—just the perfection she demanded in every aspect of her life. The room was suffocatingly still, the only sound was the rhythmic clicking of Ariana's black gel pen—a tool she had come to rely on more than she'd ever admit. The pen was sleek, thin, its black casing smooth under her fingers, as if designed to fit the shape of her hand perfectly. Each click resonated in the quiet, a sharp *tick-tick-tick* against the otherwise mute air. She clicked it again, absently this time, and it punctuated the silence, an anxious beat in the heart of the room.

Ariana's eyes were locked on the screen before her, her gaze moving quickly over the columns of Elina's spending sheet. Her fingers flew over the keys, pausing only to analyze the numbers. The data was cold, methodical—but she knew the truth was hidden within it. Each line, every transaction, felt like it could be the key to unraveling everything. Her mind sifted through it all, the financial entries as sharp and pointed as knives in her thoughts. It wasn't enough, though. She needed more—something to piece it all together, something to connect the dots that had been scattered so carelessly.

The hum of the air conditioning, barely perceptible, filled the room, adding a layer of subtle white noise that only heightened the tension. Ariana's eyes flicked to the corner of the room where Luna sat, still hunched over the papers, barely moving. Luna had become a hollow presence beside her, a mere shadow of the person she once was, eyes glazed over in an endless fog of grief. Ariana could sense Luna's detachment, the emptiness that had consumed her, and it grated at her. But Ariana had no time to focus on that now.

"Luna," Ariana said quietly, her voice cutting through the silence like a knife.

Luna didn't respond right away—just a slow blink as if the sound of her name had barely reached her. Ariana's sharp gaze never wavered from the screen.

"Get Elina's spending history for the last six months. Put it into a new column. I need everything sorted."

Luna nodded, her movement slow and almost robotic. Ariana didn't wait for her to begin—she didn't need to. The work was hers to carry, as it had always been.

Ariana clicked her pen again, the soft sound slicing through the stillness, and typed furiously, fingers moving with precision. The spreadsheet was coming together, but it was still just a mass of data. Nothing concrete. Nothing real. Her mind churned, seeking something she had missed. A soft ping from her phone broke through the focus, and she glanced at the screen: a message from her assistant in the agency.

*"Ella's meeting is scheduled for later today. Unknown contact in the studio."*

The words hit her like a jolt. *Ella.* Her heart rate quickened. The butler. There had been something nagging at her, something that felt wrong about Ella, but she hadn't been able to place it. Not yet.

Ariana let out a soft sigh, the air cool against her skin. She set her pen down and typed a quick response. *"Full surveillance on Ella. Every move, every word. Now."* Her eyes, still hard and calculating, didn't leave the screen. She could feel the weight of her breath, slow and steady, almost as if her lungs were trying to hold her together.

* * * * *

# Chapter 15

# the Betrayal of a Butler

Focusing her eyes on the door of her study room, she heard the distant sound of footsteps coming from the hallway outside. Ella was heading in the direction of the study room. Ariana's breathing hitched for a moment, she rose from the desk, her chair scraping gently across the hardwood floor. Each second she lost was another second Ella could slip away from her.

Ariana moved towards the hallway, The scent of the incense that bathed the study adhered to her, its smell rich and heavy, nearly overpowering.

As she got to the bathroom, she stopped, her ears perked up. A muted murmur entered her ears.

Ella's voice. Ariana moved closer to the bathroom door, silently, "I told you; it's nearly done. We can't pull out now. You crazy"

Ariana's heart pounded in her chest as she tried to think. Who was Ella speaking to? And what was this—"done"?

the tension hung in the air. The light aroma of lavender soap still clung to the bathroom, blending with the richer scent of the incense from the study room. The combination of scents turned Ariana's stomach acidic with discomfort. She pressed her ears harder, her fingertips grazing the cold wood of the door, a fraction of an inch short of detection.

If you do this, it'll be done. No turning back," Ella went on, her voice low but full of finality.

A scraping of a chair against the floor was heard in Ariana's ears, and then a soft laugh from the other individual on the other side of the dialogue. The responding voice was low, too muffled to separate, but the words themselves were clear enough.

"Sure about what?" What if they discover it? Ariana felt her stomach bottom out. They discover. Were they talking about the investigation, or something other than that? Her mind skittered through possibilities. It wasn't merely about Elina's death now. This was something deeper. Something evil.

"I will do whatever is needed," Ella spat, her words taking on an icy determination. "The truth no longer holds any value. Only this." Ariana's breath caught. This. It was all making sense. Whatever Ella was up to, it was larger than the investigation, larger than Elina's murder. Ariana couldn't wait any longer. She needed to know, and she needed to know now.

She moved away from the door, her own pulse still ringing in her ears. The gravity of what she had learned weighed down on her like a rock in water, falling deeper into her mind. The bathroom seemed colder, the walls seeming to close in around her as she rapidly retreated back to the study room.

As her fingers drifted over her phone, Ariana's thoughts reeled, the scheme already taking shape in her mind. She texted her assistant for the third time: "Full surveillance on Ella. No more secrets."

She couldn't wait. Not any longer.

Ariana's thoughts were already racing, the pieces of the puzzle she'd just heard clicking into place, each one cutting and evil than the next. Her hand shook slightly as she placed her phone on the desk, her fingers wandering over the smooth, cold glass Her gaze shifted over to Luna, still seated in her daze, her fingers limp as she went through the same stack of papers for what seemed like the hundredth time. Ariana couldn't afford to waste her attention on her anymore. Luna had been worthless at this time. Ariana was on her own in this. She had to be.

* * * * *

# Chapter 16

# The Pen of Secrets

She clicked the pen again, quietly, as if in an attempt to concentrate. Focusing once more on the spreadsheet in front of her on the laptop, she studied the figures again, the dates and transactions hiding before her. The tea test from the chemist yes, there it was again, that annoying sensation. The pieces of the puzzle didn't quite fit yet, but she felt they would. She required a little more to connect the dots. She was acutely sensitive to the way the tension that was prevailing. She laid her ear against the chilled wood of the door, and listened once more. Ella's voice had been gentle, but Ariana could pick up still on the faraway hum of the conversation inside.

"I don't care what it takes," Ella said, her voice firm and unyielding, though there was a hint of something evil beneath it. "We have to do this, no matter what. The time is now. It's happening."

She quietly opened the door, just a crack, to look through. She couldn't see Ella's face, but the words were distinct enough.

"I'll handle it. Everything's in place," came the reply. A pause. "You don't know what you're getting yourself into, Ella. There's no turning back once you're in."

Ariana's breath hitched. She could barely breathe as she stood frozen in place. No turning back. What had Ella gotten herself involved in? Her hand voluntarily closed over the door handle. She had to keep her reasons about her. She couldn't let this get away.

A chill crept up her spine as she pulled back from the door, her heart pounding more fiercely with every second. She moved towards the desk. Unspoken truths were haunting. Ariana leaned back in her chair, hands shaking as she picked up her phone again. She had to move fast. The pressure of the moment was crushing, each second lost.

She had to ensure Ella didn't get away from her. She typed another message. "Get me everything on Ella. Her history, her contacts, everything. Full surveillance, immediate effect."

She required a strategy. She needed to be one step ahead, to get in front of Ella and whatever game she was playing. She saw Hannah come into the room. The sight of her best friend was a welcoming relief.

"Hannah," Ariana said softly, her tone a little cooler than normal. "We have to talk. We need to go faster than I anticipated. Ella's more involved than I realized. I need to know all about her. No more delaying."

Hannah's eyebrows raised but she nodded. She recognized this was important. "Got it," she replied calmly. "I'll work on it. Next?"

Ariana's eyes shifted to the screen once more. She needed to stay one step ahead to remain in command. "We need to expose everything. Background and links all of it. Can't trust a person at present."

Hannah also nodded. Luna didn't speak, but she looked sad. "Anything else?" Hannah asked, her voice taking on a lower tone as she moved closer.

"I'm going to have to discuss this with Albert. Get him back here. I need another set of eyes on this. And watch out for Luna. She's. disappearing."

Hannah nodded again and moved towards the door. She couldn't lose any more time. She faced the screen once more, her fingers typing once again across the keyboard, opening up all the files, all the information, everything she required.

She felt the intensity of the moment is high. Her eyes shifting from one detail to the next.

And then she heard it again, the distant echo of Ella's voice. But this time, there was something more.

"I can't do it by myself. We must go quickly," Ella's voice was sharp.

Ariana's gaze shifted towards the door that had grown deeply from her childhood.

She didn't need to listen anymore. She had what she required.

She rose to her feet, walking with the confidence. Each step was the start of something new and far greater, and Ariana knew that from here on there would be no return.

* * * * *

# Chapter 17

# The Postmortem Results

Ariana rose to her feet. Her voice, which had been tentative and pale before, now recovered its authoritative taste. She stared at Luna and spoke. "Ella is in trouble. The sort we still don't fully understand. In order to find our suspect, we have to eliminate her first. We can't cross others until we've safeguarded ourselves."

Luna glared at Ariana in shock, her eyes wide.

Hannah, who had been quiet until now, spoke firmly, her voice bearing a sense of professionalism. "Today is February 8th. Tomorrow, February 9th. We have already tracked Elina's spending, and the postmortem reports will arrive. We know her eating patterns, her routines. Phase 2 begins tomorrow."

Albert walked in at that moment. He wore a sharply cut black and white suit, moving with a seemingly effortless ease. He faced them with poise, his accent rich and authoritative.

"Madame, I am at your service," he replied with his deep voice.

Ariana's gaze shifted to him, her voice steady. "Albert, get me coffee. Heavy cream."

Nodding, Albert stepped out of the room without comment.

As the door closed, Ariana's phone vibrated on the table next to her. The bold font flashed the name: Seraphina. Ariana's hands picked up the call. Seraphina's voice impatient. "The postmortem result is in, Ariana," she announced abruptly, with tension.

Ariana's eyes glanced across the room toward a black-and-red, thin cupboard. She went over to it, she opened it, drew out a blue notebook, and headed over to her computer. As she opened the notebook and booted up the computer. Ariana sat at the dark, polished wood table, her gaze sweeping over the open notebook. Her fingers moved over the keyboard, calling up the postmortem report on the screen. As the document loaded, she let out a slow breath. Her eyes dashed to Luna, who was already heading for the chemist's report laid out on the table.

"Luna," Ariana instructed, "match the chemist's findings with the postmortem. Every single detail has to match. If there is a discrepancy, it's our clue. Ensure nothing is missed."

Luna nodded quickly, her hands shaking slightly as she gathered the documents. She worked efficiently, as she riffled through the dense stack of papers, each one filled with chemical testing, toxicology reports, and autopsy results.

Hannah, who had been observing from the corner, walked over to the corkboard in the back of the room. The board was still largely empty, only a lone name written in red pen Elina. Below it, three suspects were listed, their names written in cold, exact blue.

"Elina," Ariana whispered to herself, "The secret lies in the details. We simply need to uncover it."

She rose from her seat, her eyes darting between Hannah and Luna. She indicated the corkboard. "Let's fill it in. Begin noting the noticeable points on sticky notes. color-coded. Green for personal, blue for success, and red for death."

Hannah grabbed a pile of sticky notes off the desk. Her hands drawing out the notes and positioning them beside the name Elina.

Hannah's said "Chemist report reveals trace of potassium cyanide in her blood. It's compatible with poisoning. Postmortem verifies cause of death. Acute cyanide poisoning."

Ariana's eyes narrowed, the pieces of the puzzle falling into place in her mind. "A staged death. Someone who knew precisely how to cover their trace"

Ariana added another sticky note Potassium Cyanide: Red. it said. Simultaneously, Hannah completed a green sticky note. Elina's Success: Prominent historian. She stuck it underneath the name Elina, with the green note conspicuous against the black cork board.

"Add her personal life," Ariana said. "We need every angle. Her family, friendships everything. Her personal life may provide motivation." Luna drew a file out of the pile and opened it. "Elina was married, but her husband passed away in a car accident last year. She had one close friend, Carla. There is a reference to a recent falling out with her best friend."

Another sticky note was placed, this one green. Personal Life: Widowed, falling out with close friend Carla.

As the board started filling up, the team's movements were becoming more deliberate, each of them covering ground with intent. The corkboard was being shaped, a web of red pins and sticky notes gradually revealing the life and death of Elina, one point at a time.

Albert reentered the room quietly, holding a tray with the coffee Ariana had requested.

She nodded at him without breaking her focus, taking the cup quickly.

"Phase 2 begins tomorrow," Hannah said, her tone steady as she placed the last of the notes on the board. "We'll track every suspect's movement. Every one of them could have access to cyanide."

Ariana's tone was gentle but firm. "Phase 2 isn't monitoring. We have to excavate Elina's environment further. Who will profit the most by her murder? Who had the capability to perform such an act?

Luna raised her head from the chemist's report. "But. who would do this? All three suspects had some sort of connection to her, but none of them look like they'd go this far."

"Right," Ariana said, narrowing her eyes. "That's the issue.". We must see past what they wish us to observe. Ariana stood at the desk, reading over the report before her. The evidence was thin. She'd been awake for hours, but sleep was a distant dream for her now. Luna, still staining the remaining traces of tears from her eyes, hesitated. She appeared as though she were about to question something but not sure whether or not to proceed. Ariana instructed Luna. "Luna, tomorrow, you'll escort Lavinia and Julian in for me. You'll assist.

Luna's voice shook. "For what?"

"The investigation," Ariana answered, her gaze shifting back to the report. "Read it. Elina was healthy prior to the poisoning. But the cyanide. It was more powerful this time. More intense." She waited for a moment. "We don't have much time, Luna.

Luna blinked back another wave of tear and seemed exhausted. She nodded and spoke. "I'll be there," she said quietly, voice stressed.

Ariana was not a sympathizer, but she could recognize Luna was hanging on by threads. "Go home," she told her quietly but firmly. "It's late. 9:30 already. Go to bed. We'll have to have you sharp on time here tomorrow."

Without speaking, Luna turned and walked toward the door. The night air slapped

Luna in the face, but it could not scatter the thoughts shaking in her head. She glanced up at the sky and stars. She slid into a yellow and black cab without looking back. How had she overlooked something? The idea overwhelmed her, but they don't have time now. Back in the building, Ariana exhaled deeply. She scanned the report pages again, searching for anything that would help explain Elina's poisoning. It was too neat, too deliberate. Someone had thought this out.

Ariana and Hannah had tacked the increasing pile of evidence. The pictures of Elina, the toxicology results, the witness accounts, all scattered about a fractured puzzle that would not come together. No matter how hard they tried, the pieces doesn't seem to fit. Not yet.

Ariana stood fixed in front of the board, gazing at the papers on it which is reminding her constantly that Elina's case was getting away from them. Hannah sat on the floor, coffee mug in her hand, turning the pages of a stack of papers they'd pulled from Elina's research libraries. There were notes on the Dor crown. Elina's life's work, her passion, her specialty. There was beauty in the writing, Hannah said. Each word carefully chosen, each sentence poised with historical accuracy.

"You're lost in thought again," Hannah said, filling the silence. "What are you thinking about, Ariana?"

Ariana's gaze rushed to the papers on the floor, then back to the corkboard. "See how Elina described the Dors," Ariana whispered, gesturing towards the page held by Hannah. "She had this fixation about their power dynamics, how the monarchy was established on lies, betrayal, and domination. She chose every single word, just like a chess game thinking ahead, planned, always making a few moves at a time."

Hannah seen examining the pages once more. "Yes, but how does that relate to a poisoned woman and an absent culprit?".

* * * * *

# Chapter 18

# The Unexpected Surprise

Ariana breathed slowly, her hand tracing the border of a photograph stuck to the board, a photo of Elina at a conference, beside an older historian. She was smiling, but Ariana could detect the tension in her eyes. A front. A photo thoroughly put together to hide something beneath.

"It's the way she thought," Ariana explained,

"Elina didn't only study history. She studied it analytically, observing people, anticipating their actions. Her research on the Dors wasn't academic. It was a lens through which she saw the world. She wasn't studying power. She was learning how to control it."

Hannah asked, "You believe she saw herself within the Dors? Or worse someone else did?

Someone who used what they had learned to her disadvantage?"

Ariana saw the pile of papers scattered upon the table. "Yes," she whispered. "I believe somebody caught a glimpse of that part of her. Someone who knew the way she worked, thought."

She didn't know where the pieces had originated, but now they were falling into place in a manner that was almost too disturbing.

Hannah stood up and said "So, you're saying Elina was a target all along. Someone who knew how to read her. like an open book."

Ariana's eyes never left the board. "Exactly. Whatever they did here, they were watching her. Observing her mind work, the way she observed history. They knew everything about her vulnerabilities, her thinking, her innocence. They could have manipulated her like a pawn".

But it wasn't only about the evidence. it was about realizing how Elina had lived her life, how her mind had been her best tool and her worst enemy. She'd learned history, but she'd never really realized how history could repeat itself in a manner that would kill her.

Hannah went over and stood beside Ariana, scanning the board a final time. "It's all in her words," she said. "Her papers. Her research. If we know how she thought, we know what happened."

Ariana nodded gradually. "The key was right there, her work on the Dors wasn't just academic. It was how Elina understood the world. If she could grasp the way Elina viewed people, she might understand how the killer moved, how they thought".

Abruptly, the door opened. Albert, the butler, slipped in without a sound. His arrival was always silent, as if he were a ghost, but tonight there was something in his eyes that gave Ariana pause. He had been observing them in the shadows for days, dropping mysterious hints now and then, but never taking action.

Albert's eyes darted to the corkboard, and then returned to Ariana. "I see you're getting somewhere," he murmured. "But maybe it's time to take a step back. Your therapist wishes you leave the case"

Ariana's eyebrows narrowed "What do you mean, she wants me to leave the case?

Hannah moved deeper into the room. "Sometimes, the solution is right in front of you. We've been concentrating on the wrong pieces." Her gaze drifted to the pages of Elina's Dor studies, then to the photos lying on the board. "Do not look at the events themselves, but at how Elina viewed them. How she understood the world. You may discover your solution in her mind, not in the facts."

Silently, Ariana turned back to the corkboard, her mind flashing between the remains of evidence, her attention narrowing. Looking at the photo of Elina, at the pages of Dor history she had once written, it clicked. Ariana's eyes became alert. "It's all a matter of how Elina perceived her enemies. She described their tactics—how they conquered battles not through violence, but manipulation, through the right words, the right movements.

Whoever did this employ the same tactic against her. She didn't have to beat her down. She had to dominate her mind."

There was a silence in the room as Ariana turned to Hannah. "It was someone who knew how to manipulate her. Someone she trusted, perhaps even looked up to. They didn't have to poison her directly. They poisoned her mind first."

Hannah exhaled slowly. "And then it was too late". Ariana sat at the table, viewing the corkboard before her, eyes weighed down with fatigue. The pieces they'd gathered in the last several hours were beginning to add up. Slowly. But there was so much more to learn yet.

Her fingers ran over the map of Elina's papers on the Dors, it was more than six hours since they had started working, beginning at ten the night before, now nearing four in the morning and her eyes ached from fatigue. Hannah was dozing in her seat, her head leaning against the desk, her eyes barely open.

Ariana didn't have the option to pause.

Her phone abruptly buzzed on the table, Ariana rapidly picked it up, looking at the screen. The name in the caller ID sent a cold shiver through her. Lavinia.

She touched the screen, lifting the phone to her ear. "Lavinia? What's wrong?"

There was a hesitant silence on the other line, then the unmistakable voice of Lavinia gentle and shaking.

"Ariana. Luna. Luna's dead. She was killed. Last night."

"Lavinia," she was able to whisper, her voice shaking and low. "Where? What happened?"

"They discovered her this morning," Lavinia said, gritting her teeth to keep her composure. "In the manor house. Nobody is sure who killed her yet." Her voice cracked, and she halted. "It was a dagger, Ariana."

Ariana's heart missed a beat. She couldn't even get her head around it. "I'm coming over. You stay there."

The phone hung up, and Ariana sat silently, frozen for an instant. Luna, killed. It was not supposed to end like that. She still could picture her, crying, begging to know why she was brought into it, so thin and lost. And now dead. The image curled her stomach.

Ariana jumped up, looking at Hannah, who was still dazed. She shook her awake. "Hannah, wake up. We have to leave."

"What? What's going on?" Hannah groggily opened her eyes.

"It's Luna. She's dead. She was killed." The words were spoken in a soft whisper, but the effect was instantaneous. Hannah's eyes opened wide as the truth sank in. "Luna?" she said. "No... No, this can't be".

Ariana snatched her coat, hastening, she did not hesitate to pick up her keys and move toward her Rolls-Royce, her mind racing. The engine roared as she started the car, a swift, soothing purr amidst the suffocating quiet. The ride was a haze. Each passing moment took what seemed like forever as her mind continued to rewind and fast-forward over Luna. what did she do? Why Luna? Had she gotten close to the truth?

Her hands clutched the steering wheel tighter.

It felt too wrong.

As she navigated the streets to Lavinia's house, the dashboard clock flashed 4:15 AM. The blackness outside engulfed the car, the streetlights flashing an unforgiving, hollow light. She stepped on the gas pedal more firmly, the tires slicing through the night with urgency.

As she came to the manor, it was like entering a house in time twist. The house stood before her, big and dark, against the backdrop of the night sky. The only noise was the wind rustling through the trees. The stone front appeared unreal, as if a tomb.

Ariana got out of the car, her heels clacking on the driveway gravel. She was hardly noticing anything around her. The only thing that mattered was Luna, somewhere within that house, her life lost to the chill steel of a dagger.

Lavinia was at the door, her face gray, her eyes far away. The look on her face startled

Ariana, but she suppressed it for the time being.

"Lavinia," Ariana said softly, approaching her. "Tell me everything."

"They. they discovered her in the study," Lavinia whispered, her voice cracking. "There was no evidence of a struggle, but. but they believe she knew her murderer. She was stabbed. It wasn't random."

Ariana's blood ran cold. "The person who did this knew her."

Lavinia nodded, tears brimming in her eyes. "Yes."

The house was quiet now, aside from the sound of faraway footsteps and subdued voices of the staff, attempting to comprehend the tragedy.

Ariana and Lavinia made their way through the corridors until they came to the study. Luna's dead body lay sprawled on the floor, blood spreading around her. The dagger still remained deep in her chest, its hilt shining with the dim light. The room seemed to be in a state of immaculateness, except for the brutality that had been let loose within.

Ariana's stomach turned, but she forced herself to focus. This wasn't about her feelings. It was about Luna's death. Someone in this house had done this.

She took her phone out of her pocket and dialed the number that was memorized. The line rang twice before the crisp voice on the other end answered.

"Maya Wren," the voice said.

"It's Ariana," she said, her voice firm "There's a new situation. Luna's been killed. I want you to get over here. Bring the team."

Maya was silent for a long moment. "I'm on my way."

The line went dead, and Ariana turned to Lavinia, who stood frozen, her eyes wide and unblinking. "We'll get justice for Luna," Ariana said firmly, although she wasn't sure if she believed it herself.

Inside a few minutes came Maya Wren, hot on the heels of Sebastian Crove, Benedict Thornfield, and Seraphina Sunfield, they entered in pairs, their expression somber as they gazed upon the site. With every new entrant, the air grew more laden, Luna's death weighing in Ariana's heart all the more.

The detectives quickly got to work, their trained eyes measuring the room, trying to reconstruct what had occurred. Maya knelt beside Luna's body, studying the wound with clinical detachment. The rest of the team spread out, scanning the room for signs of break-in or other evidence.

"She was stabbed with a dagger," Maya replied after a moment of silence, her tone low and level. "But not any dagger. This one features a particular pattern an older model. It's not a typical weapon."

Ariana's thoughts were keen.

"Would it have been something personal? Somebody who was familiar with Luna enough that they'd select a weapon such as this?"

Maya nodded slowly. "Maybe. This wasn't random. It was intimate."

As the team started to search the room, Benedict called out from the corner. "There are no struggle signs other than the body itself. She wasn't surprised. Whoever did this have control."

Seraphina observed the windows. "The room wasn't tampered with. It's as if the killer had the precision to enter and leave without being seen."

The team remained in silence for a brief moment. They all recognized the seriousness of what had emerged.

"Get Luna's body to the mortuary for postmortem," Ariana cracked, "We need to know it all. This cannot remain unsolved." The room became rigid and quiet as the team went into motion.

Ariana took a moment to stand back, still racing with her mind. The killer was loose out there, and they were nearer than ever.

But the idea is Luna had been right on the edge of the truth. And now she was dead.

* * * * *

# Chapter 19

# **Unraveling Secrets**

Rain hitting the windows was the only thing that was with Ariana when she was in the middle of the of the Baxter estate.

Luna, the second eldest sister of the Baxter family, was dead.

The police were the first to arrive, and the body was already in the cooler room. Luna's corpse remained on the cold, stony floor of the library, a shaking contrast to the warmth of the fire that had burned only a few hours before. She couldn't get rid of the sense that something greater than the horror of Luna's death was coming apart here.

The dagger remained, stuck deep in Luna's chest, the blood coming around it. It was cruel and efficient, and it left no doubt that her death was not accident. The only thing left to know now was who had done this, and why.

Ariana entered the room. The detectives, Maya, Sebastian, Benedict, and Seraphina, were summoned straight away. They were standing around the room, taking notes, staring at the dagger. But Ariana's gaze fell on Luna's lifeless body. She was still so young. So vibrant. How could anyone has harmed her like this?

"Is everything okay?" Ariana's voice broke the silence.

Maya Wren, the least skilled of the group, glanced up. "All fits the initial indications. No struggle. The dagger. it's spotless. It's surgical." She hesitated, looking now as she inspected the weapon again. "It's too clean. Whoever performed this was absolutely certain of what they were doing."

Ariana looked at the complicated, gemstone covered handle of the dagger. "Who would have access to a dagger like that?". "Someone close," Benedict said, his voice guarded. "Someone who has been in this house before. Someone with money, status. and maybe, power."

Ariana did not have time to think over them. The press had descended upon them. The flashing lights from outside the mansion had started piercing the windows, and the media were persistent in their search for answers. They were hungry for a headline, any headline, that would provide them with something to run with.

"We must treat this sensitively," Seraphina said, her white face turned towards the door. "There are reporters outside. They won't leave us alone." She couldn't possibly retreat now. She had to meet them head-on. The front gates of the Baxter mansion wide opened, and at once, the camera flashes blinded her. Reporters shouted her name, firing questions she had no response to. "Ariana! Was Luna's death an accident? Did she take part in any risky activities lately?". She was standing tall, her eyes breaking, her manner authoritative. The journalists attempted to shout over one another, bringing microphones into her face, but Ariana did not back down.

"It wasn't an accident," she declared. "Luna was killed. One moved forward, her tone energetic and demanding. "Do you have any suspects? Was Luna involved in any recent altercations? Maybe within the family?"

Ariana's eyes laid-back. She had known this was coming. The questions regarding the family. The probing into each relationship. But she could not let them take over. Not now.

"There are so many things we still don't know. I'm talking to my team in order to find out the truth," Ariana declared, speaking firmly but calmly. "This was no accident. But until we know more, I beg you to be patient."

A journalist raised their microphone. "Do you think that the murder was related to the history of the family? Is this a matter of inheritance or family rivalry?

Ariana's eyes raised. The Baxter's' past was no trivial affair. It was a family founded upon money and strength, and power tended to create its own kill or be-killed games. But she refused to let someone else set the story. Not until she'd heard all her facts.

"We're still probing," Ariana replied. "There's more involved in this case than anyone yet knows, but at present I can say nothing more."

She turned away from the press, her glance darting to Hannah, who had remained by her side throughout this catastrophe. Ariana shot one final glance at the crowd of press before entering the house. "Let's get back to work," she said to her team, her voice firm. The search was just starting. Inside, the air smelt of wood, dust, and old coffee. The team jumped into action. Ariana marched straight to the corkboard on the corner of the study, a spontaneous map of their investigation. The board was a chaos of photos, documents, and scribbles, all of which created a disjointed picture of Luna's last days. "We must concentrate," she told Maya and Sarah. "What do we definitely know?"

Maya started reading the case history which she wrote. "Luna had a dagger pushed into her chest. Clean kill, no battle. She did not protect herself. The assassin must have been someone she knew."

Benedict joined in, adding his observations. "The dagger is old. Likely a family inheritance. I've seen something like it in the royal collection, but it's usually locked away. Only a few people in the house would have access to it."

Ariana shot a surprised look at the dagger then slowly drifted her attention

"Who are those people?" Ariana asked. "Lavinia," Maya said first. "She's the third youngest, and she's been close to Luna. Julian. He's the youngest, but he's protective of her. And Isolde, she's. well, Isolde. But I've never seen her with that dagger. She doesn't strike me as someone who would know how to use it."

Ariana nodded, committing the facts to memory. She couldn't help but remember Isolde, Luna and Elina's little sister had always been an unfriendly presence in the family. She'd never gotten along with Luna, though she'd appeared to accept her younger siblings.

Nevertheless, Ariana couldn't help but notice the peculiar tension between them.

"I'll speak to them later," Ariana replied. "Let's just deal with the house for now. We need to know who was here last night, who had access to Luna's room."

Seraphina looked up from her notes. "I discovered something strange in Luna's journal. It's a note regarding a meeting. She was to meet someone in the library at ten last night, but there's no name. She writes it as if it's someone she knows."

Ariana became slightly more suspicious "Who might she have been meeting?"

"I don't know," Seraphina replied, raising her brow. "But it's something we have to investigate.

As the squad started to snoop around the rest of the house, they found more parts of the puzzle. It wasn't only the death of Luna that they had to solve. There were layers of lies, power struggles, and family secrets. Something had been going on with Luna.

She had been onto something, something evil enough to get someone killed.

They had found the weapon, the note, and the strained relationships. But now, as Ariana followed the detectives from one room to the next. Each step they took them closer to an answer, but there were too many questions. Who had murdered Luna? And more pressing still, why?

Hours went by. It was almost 6 a.m. when Ariana and her crew were ready to take a break at last. They had covered the corkboard with all the clues they had discovered. Luna's diary entries, snapshots of individuals who had been in and out of the house, the cryptic meeting note. And then, as Ariana settled into the desk chair, something caught her attention.

A picture, an ancient one of Luna with some man she'd never met before. The fellow was standing at her back, just out of focus in the background of some family reunion.

"This can't be," Ariana spoke softly to herself, bringing the photo closer to her eyes. She'd never met this man before, yet he was near enough to Luna that she had been photographed beside him.

"I found something," Ariana whispered, her voice low and urgent.

Hannah moved over to her and saw that photo and said "Who is he?"

"I don't know," Ariana exclaimed. "But this is a new clue. We have to discover who this man is.". "By the time the dawn crept across the estate, Ariana was certain of one thing. Luna's death was a message too. Each response they found only led to more, and she felt the pressure of the investigation going high. Albert entered and announced "Madam Clara Jackson would like to speak with you about the history of the Carons". She hesitated for a moment and considered the 'dark history of the carons was going to be pulled into the light'. She entered the living room.

* * * * *

# Chapter 20

# The Dark Truth of Carons (Ariana Caron's Ancestry)

Ariana sat back as Clara's pen hovered on her notebook. Each word spoken drawing Clara deeper into the maze of power, manipulation, and ruthless strategy that defined the Caron family legacy.

The query had been straightforward. How did the Carons gain control of such huge money? How did a family with so much nobility receive its title or noble blood in the first place become so powerful?

Ariana's smiled, but her eyes flashed a brief glimpse of something else. A woman considered down by her history, by the legacy of what had been hers. She did not say anything for a moment, letting the silence hang between them.

"Well, Clara, in order to know the Carons, you have to know how we came up and why, more so," she started softly. "We inherited our fortune. We created it. And we created it by playing at a game no one else knew.

Clara waited with pen in hand, ready to capture each word. Ariana went on, to tell the story which is something long ago, something lost to the ages.

"The Caron family's first real test came in the 5th century. France at the time was a land of chaos. The collapse of the Roman Empire had left a power vacuum, with numerous groups competing for power. The Carons were aristocrats. We were traders, mercenaries, Advisors, nobles etc. We knew that in such a world, only the strongest and the cleverest would survive."

"But it was at the games that we really came into our own. The killing games."

Clara's brow rose, her interest sparked. "Killing games?"

Ariana nodded, her face grim.

"Yes. These were not sport games. These were the games of power, of survival. And they were played at the highest level. We referred to them as Jeux d'heritage"

"The first game we played was L'Ascension, which means 'The Ascent.' After the fall of the Roman Empire, there were no obvious leaders." Each man, each family, was competing for land, power, and dominance. The Carons-a noble aristocratic class of counselors at the time started to make their move. They understood that they could never advance in the classical way by force. No. We did a game of influence, placing ourselves with the proper connections. The twist was that associations were weak at the time, and as often deadly as foes.

You see, the one rule of L'Ascension was that no one could be trusted. The temporary alliances that were made were always with the understanding that betrayal was a possibility. The game was easy become powerful, acquire land, amass wealth but always, always have an escape plan. The moment you trusted someone completely, the game was lost. And those who lost? They were discarded, exiled, or worse murdered.

Clara jotted down a note, her thoughts racing with the consequences. But Ariana's voice didn't hesitate. She was master of the tale, and she would continue until the entire picture of the story got painted.

"The second game," Ariana went on, "was entitled Le Pari de Fer meaning The Iron Bet.' As the Carons established themselves as rulers of the area, it was apparent that riches were no longer a matter of land or crowds. It was a matter of resources. And there was no more valuable resource than iron. The Carons, even the planners, knew that whoever owned the iron trade owned the future.". This game was not about alliances. It was about influence and handling. Iron was the blood of the kingdom, and we saw to it that we controlled the mines, the supply chain, which is the very core of France's military strength.

Ariana's eyes sparkled, as if recalling the rush of victory. "We took the initiative, becoming major players in the iron industry.".

We practiced the Iron Bet by keeping our rivals one step behind undermining their transactions, derailing their cargos. But we did it secretly, behind the scenes, while pretending to be nothing more than nobles obtaining through justice. The trick was not to appear a threat.

Clara's pen moved rapidly across the page

Ariana went on, "The third game, the one that would really establish the Caron legacy, was known as La Danse des Ombres, or The Dance of Shadows.' This game was not about iron, territory, or even diplomacy. It was about perception, about getting people to see you in one way while keeping your real power out of sight in the shadows. It started during the BCE era when our power began to expand among the French nobility.". We had already conquered the art of commerce, but now it was time to conquer the art of politics."

"We manipulated the attitudes of the powerful into thinking we were just nobles, content to play their games. But secretly, we dictated all from behind the scenes.

Marriages, appointments, and even the laws themselves that ruled the land. We were universal, influencing every choice. But nobody realized it. And that was the genius of it."

Clara sat there in stunned silence as she listened to Ariana. "The Carons ruled France in the shadows. And we still do.". But La Danse des Ombres didn't stop with politics. It became something more. A sequence of games manipulating every facet of society from marriages to businesses to even royal appointments. They knew that wealth was merely a by-product of control."

Clara's froze was seen. Ariana was saying. "And you played these games as well?"

Ariana nodded.

"I was taught to play from the time I was able to understand. I was forced to learn the rules. How to control perception, how to outsmart everyone, how to be quiet but strong.

"And when did you take over?" Clara whispered.

Ariana sat back in her chair; her eyes unblinking. "When my father passed away. I inherited his big portion. Played the games and his job. My siblings were called dumb."

she went on. "But those who play the legacy games don't win only through strategy. They win through the force of history. You see, Clara, the Carons were never more than a family. They were a dynasty, and most of the dynasties were constructed out of manipulation, strategy, and calculated, measured moves.

Every step is a calculation. You never reveal your hand, and you never trust anyone. Unless you have no other option. "And you always, always have the option to make another person pay for your errors."

She smiled very slightly, a shadow moving across her face.

"Do you think the Carons' legacy is all about money? It's not. It's about having the power to control, to make people do what you want them to do. You can be the wealthiest person in the world, but without control, you have nothing."

Clara remained motionless. All of her family's past, all of their moves, their betrayals everything was part of a legacy, a set of fatal games which had been played out over centuries. And now, Ariana was the mistress of them all.

"And now, Clara, you understand the truth. The Caron legacy wasn't constructed on mere wealth. It was constructed on games. Games played with brains, with cruelty and these games were never ceased. Clara, who sat facing her, was waiting. Waiting for the truth.

"You want to know what it takes to inherit everything, Clara?"

"I'll tell you." Clara leaned in.

"'The Caron family,'" Ariana started, her voice calm, "has dominated immense wealth and power for more than a thousand years. We were born into royalty. We constructed our empire from the ruins of a dying world. My people knew something the rest of Europe did not. It was never about wealth or power. It was about control. Control of information and perception of lives."

It all started after the Roman Empire fell. Europe was in disarray nobody knew who was in charge, who to trust. But not the Carons. We knew that power could be gained without a sword. The mind was the deadliest weapon of all. When I was young, I read a lot of books about the mind.

"From the 5th century onwards, the Carons became masters of manipulation. We were taught from the beginning that wealth and power weren't things you possessed. They were things you managed, things you acquired through planning and farsightedness. Not through fight, but through the brain."

Clara remained quiet. My father, Lucien Caron II, was the one who took that legacy and made it something unimaginable," Ariana went on. "He understood how to make people feel like they were in charge when in fact they were nothing more than pawns. He manipulated the monarchy, the courts, and the rich families of France. He employed marriage, alliances, and backroom deals to make the Caron name be associated with power.

"And then he died, leaving me to inherit everything."

"But it wasn't easy, Clara,"

"Lucien left me no peaceful legacy," she said. "There were enemies. There were others who believed they could have what was mine". Especially My sister, Isabella. Isabella has hard feelings about all the Carons. She was never interested in our money. She disliked the games we played, the manipulation, the domination. She wanted none of it.

"Isabella was never the first challenge. The middle child, the second heir. But she was weak. She doesn't know what had to be done. So, when my father passed away, she fled the family. And in that moment, I knew it was my game to win."

"I observed my father for years. How he manipulated, how he played people against one another. But I played my cards differently. I knew the world was evolving, that the old ways were no longer sufficient. I had to be more than a silent power in the background. I had to take control of everything."

"And then the last stroke. I outsmarted my family, my cousins, even the royal eldest itself. I manipulated my grandparents, seized control of all key assets. I controlled the industries they required, the trade routes they relied on. They didn't see it coming.". She wasn't arrogant. She was simply telling the truth.

"The rest of my family, they were nothing to me. My brother, Jenneld was simple, uncompromising, believing he could alter the family history. He didn't realize that to control, you had to give up your passion. Isabella had already lost, but Jenneld? He would have stood a chance at inheriting if he'd learned to play the game. But he didn't. He was too trusting and soft. Skye one of my cousins heaved him off the caron estate during the first game, I saved him. The seriousness of Ariana's words finally registering. "And you? How did you—"

"I played the game. I employed all that my father had taught me. And now I have it all. I own the Caron Trust, the businesses, and the holdings in Europe and the world. I possess everything. And no one can steal it away from me."

You want to know how I managed it? It wasn't all about tricking them. It was about people. People's needs. People's weaknesses. I made them believe they were the ones in charge when, in fact, I was always ahead."

"I'm the last of my line now, Clara," Ariana continued,". "The last Caron, the first and last heir to everything. And I'll make sure no one ever takes it from me. This empire I've built? It's mine.

What everybody would view me as is an evil monster but I had to play them, they threatened to kill my family if I didn't therefore I and Jenneld played the 350th generation games where I won I couldn't give away my money although I earn a lot of money working as a detective I can't give away my caron allowance to someone other than myself this is a rule of caron"

I was compelled to play as I was eldest. Ariana went on. I teamed up with no one in the first game so I didn't have to betray anybody so I got 60,000 billion in my pot. Then for the second game. I tricked Skye. I used later onwards and also survived the third game. I used a map and a compass rather than gold and silver and I discovered the caron vault I used reasons threw comfort so I killed no one and received the entire money"

Ariana stood up from her seat and moved toward a silver and emerald green cabinet which had glass organizers not the pen holders but glass holders for jewels and weapons she pulled open a drawer and removed a neat rolled cloth opened the cloth there was a shield with 4 colors different from each other silver emerald green deep burgundy and gold in the middle there was a black falcon in the middle

Ariana was a bit confident and said "This is the house crest and the motto is Per l'avenir, au sommet meaning "To the future, to the summit."".

Ms. Ariana your name is Caron. Clara added.

Ariana proudly asserted we call ourselves caron

"We are considered great because of our intelligence we acquired Greece, Rome and

France fostering military alliances distributing its great origin we are brutal only with reference to success otherwise we are indeed great and we have never acted in a dishonest attitude "

Ariana Caron was a queen in her own game, and she would do whatever it took to keep what was hers.

* * * * *

# Chapter 21

# The Realization of Chess

Ariana was drained and scared most possibly for the first time since she expected Skye to push her off

John michelaar, the advocate ran front and seemed to be reading his notes on the case

Isolde was comforting lavinia and julian as she sat by their side

Hannah got an old cork board while the rest filled up files with information no one was idle however Ariana found it familiar for some reason. The caron games housing dorm. The first day morning Ariana was reading a book about partnership in chess

She shouted bravely "everyone come here I have a plan". Not even isolde continued her work she pulled julian and lavinia to a remaining blank spot

I know how to get the case done it is simple she added with a smirk; she showed a long whiteboard Ariana said

Ariana shot a cold stare at everyone making them go straight up and open a notebook with a pen so

"Elina loved the Dors thanks to their betrayal and blood which is the way she perceived the world. Elina's reports show it. Luna was kind and naive unlike Elina with a lack of conferences. She was the one wishing the family was united now we play using the suspects mind so we know Sinclair is not a suspect but someone else is and they are not Elina's nor Luna's friend, it is someone so deep who etched scars on luna making her too naive which made Elina stand up where she lost and perceives the world in this way, in her personal notebook she calls

"Failure in something, success in another". People who were in oxford course: history of monarchies, the same year as her who are also in Elina's community would be the murderer"

Everyone stared at her in shock. Hannah commanded "albert get another cork board" albert ran up, while maya asked "Ariana are you sure in your plan" Ariana coolly responded

"Maya, I have played perfectly with inheritance and power before this should be no big deal for me"

"Right" maya muttered under her breath

Ariana shouted

"detectives come here please so you see she used the remote to on a projector this is murderer clue chess so in this game there are borders the queen is the detective the king is murdered the queen must cross borders and get 5 people wisely as if she lacks information or preparation the opponents will kill her we are in such a game now we have finished a bishop luna by sending it across the borders with no preparation which is our demise or la perte de l'évêque now we discovered a spy pawn Ella or Epsion sur pion among us we kick ella is what everyone does and use our pawns to play the game we prepare but we don't push the pawn instead we take the pawns controlling device her phone and track the information that is what I would do then distance her from matters is how I would win the game now we have one clue, track Ella's calls."

Seraphina stood up and asked anything else Ariana smirked once more and spoke

Nothing should go wrong no sympathy we issue a warrant to investigate every place we can do something to prevent a disaster

Hannah strode into the attic while the rest opened their case notebooks all dark green with Ariana's detective agency logo on it

And quickly discussed in a quiet silence

* * * * *

# Chapter 22

# The Precise Score Board

Ariana Caron's mansion filled with smell of old leather and freshly made coffee. Everything boiling, ready to blow. Ariana sat in her study room where the Elina Baxter Case lay out before her, its pages covered in notes, photographs, and mysterious messages. Her keen eyes scanned the files. Elina's background, Luna's untimely death, and the scraps of information scattered on the pages each one giving a little hint, but no whole answer.

Her fingers dashed across the surface of the papers. Ariana did not bother to look up as she heard the quiet footsteps behind her. Maya Wren came. She waited at the door, expectant of being noticed.

Have you talked to Benedict yet?" Ariana's voice was a gentle command, her eyes never leaving the report she was reading.

"Yes, he's going over the security tapes of the Baxter estate again. We still can't get anything solid on the night Luna died. But we're getting closer," Maya replied and placing a thick folder on the desk. It was filled with Luna's private life journals, photos, even some receipts and notes she had taken from her sessions with Elina.

Ariana hardly noticed the folder. She pulled out another file from the drawer next to her Isolde's explanation, the facts establishing her whereabouts during both murders. "It doesn't add up," Ariana whispered.

"Luna and Elina were both murdered, and yet nobody can join the dots. Ariana's fingers trembled over the fat pile of papers. She breathed slowly, deliberately. but her face was as calm. "This was no random act," Ariana said, at last looking up to meet Maya's eyes. "Whoever did this both of these murders had an aim. It's a message, but for whom?"

Maya glanced down at the table, at the photos and notes spread in front of them. "We're missing something. A pattern."

Ariana's keen gaze flashed back to Luna's report. There was one thing that kept jumping out at her, something she just couldn't push aside. A fact she couldn't shake. Luna had been incredibly secretive in the final weeks leading up to her death. It was reported that Luna was actually searching for something concerning Elina's history research or something regarding her own family. Had something significant been discovered by Luna, something that made her a target?

Seraphina Sunfield followed, her face as stern as ever. She had been pouring over case reports with Sebastian Crove. "We've assembled everything from the Baxter estate surveillance," she said, her tone icy and crisp. "There are gaps. key gaps but, I believe there is something we overlooked.

Ariana instinctively changed her attention. She gestured to Seraphina to continue, leaning forward.

"There's this last feed that we haven't reviewed. It's a faulty recording, but I think we should check," Seraphina went on. "It was taken on the night Luna died. We have a figure off in the background, but it's just so uncertain you can hardly make them out."

Get me that tape. Now," Ariana broke.

Seraphina departed right away. Ariana did not waste a moment. She returned to Elina's folder and flipped swiftly through the most recent reports. Dialogues between Luna and Elina, held over the past few months that is tracked by tapping their phone. There was something here hidden in these dialogues. Ariana's fingers ran the edge of a page, on which Luna had said: "Don't let her find out." But what? And whom did she mean?

Abruptly Sebastian Crove was present in the room. He remained quietly by the door, holding back. He was not a man to intrude, but he was an essential presence, always monitoring every detail.

"You have anything on Isolde?" Ariana inquired. Sebastian stood holding a folder, his expression mysterious. "She's clean. No link to either murder. No motive. She wasn't even in town at the time of either death."

Ariana nodded slowly; her gaze fixed on the papers in front of her. "Then why do I think she's the key to this?". Sebastian inquired, "What do you mean?"

Ariana's eyes shined with the intensity of someone who had already solved it, but hadn't said the last word. "Something to do with Isolde's position as a middle child, the one that could never shine. There's something she envied. What if she envied her sisters, or even envied Elina's position within the family?"

Before he could reply, the knock on the door came.

Maya glanced up. "We're getting that footage," she said, and in that moment, the room seemed to hold its breath. Everyone knew that the pieces were nearly in place. The tension that had been building in every corner of Ariana's house was about to break.

Ariana rose "It's time. Let's go."

As they all exited the study room.

Ariana was prepared. She was always prepared.

* * * * *

# Chapter 23

# **Beneath the Veil of Grace**

The Rolls Royce roared to a halt before the entrance of Sinclair's Mansion, its sleek black surface looked royal. The mansion stood before them front a tapestry of grey stone, ivy climbing high into its upper tiers. Ariana Caron emerged from the car first, her tall, poised form, the line of her tailored coat sweeping over the gravel with a quiet whisper. The manor itself was a large estate, situated on a piece of land that appeared to vanish into the mist. The gentle light of lanterns illuminated the path. The great entrance hall reached high, its ceilings filled with woodwork and huge chandeliers. The floor was marble, glass-smooth, reflecting the faint light of the hallway. The walls adorned with oil paintings of ancestors as Ariana and Seraphina Sunfield stepped in. Seraphina scanned the room "It's nearly too perfect," she whispered. The scent of lavender and old wood hung in the air. "Perhaps it's all about appearances," Ariana said. She stepped forward as she led Seraphina into the living room. Her presence, even silent, was authoritative. The living room opened before them. The walls were hung with rich tapestries. There was a big fireplace at one end, but it was empty. Elegant furniture, ivory and rich mahogany stood around the room.

There was a peaceful quality to the room. Ariana, ever watchful, turned towards the tiny bar cart by the window. Pot of hot coffee was there. Its aroma was light. As she filled a cup, the heat from the ceramic mug soaked into her fingers. The coffee was bitter. The flavor clung to her tongue.

Each thing about this space the room, the coffee quietly spoke to her. Seraphina's eyes sweeping around the room, she was the first to break the silence. "It's almost too good, don't you think? It seems too planned out?"

Ariana placed her cup on the glass table. "Planned, yes. It's all set up.". Seraphina nodded,

"Too clean. Too perfect. "Yes, it's like the house has never known a change in decades. As if all has been kept still. Ariana's face remained impassive. "Come in," she said firmly.

The door open to show Sinclair standing in the doorway. His face was gentle with age. He was the epitome of elegance and poise, his modified suit perfect, his posture flawless.

He entered the room with the confidence. His eyes immediately falling on the two women.

"Ariana, Seraphina," Sinclair said. And yet, there was tension underlying his words. something unsaid hovering between them. "I wasn't looking for you today."

Ariana without any smile continued. "We have some questions, Sinclair. I hope you won't object to answering them".

"Of course. But maybe we can sit first, have a cup of coffee, while we talk?"

"You know that we don't have enough time," Ariana said. Sinclair poured himself a cup. He took a sip, then set the mug down beside him. "You're not here for coffee, Ariana. So, let's get to it."

Ariana's gaze never wavered. She took another sip of her own coffee, "Let's talk about Elina Baxter."

Each response Sinclair made only charged them deeper into silence. The last interaction that Elina Baxter shared with Sinclair prior to her demise still echoed within Ariana's mind, in bits.

The clock ticked away.

*  *  *  *  *

# Chapter 24

# Beneath the Papers

The walls of the manor seemed to close in on them as the discussion became muted. Sinclair sat opposite Ariana and Seraphina. The room was silent. "Elina talked to you last, didn't she?" Ariana's tone was low. "You were with her at that Royal Tea Party. You two discussed something." It was not a question. It was a statement of fact.

Sinclair's eyes flashed briefly, and he sipped slowly at his coffee

"Yes," he replied in a soft tone. "We did. It was an understated discussion."

Ariana's look was unyielding. "About what?"

Sinclair didn't blink. His gaze never wavered. "The Dor dynasty," he answered.

Seraphina's repeated. "The Dors?

Ariana's eyes flashed to her for a moment, then returned to Sinclair. "Elina was obsessed on them. History, the way it was presented, the way it was supposed to be presented, was her interest. She talked about how much she'd been reading lately papers, books… discussions with her closest friends. Was that you?"

"Indeed," said Sinclair. His tone softening ever so slightly as he went on. "We talked a great deal about history namely the Dors". She was especially interested in how they played power and secrets. The ability of the monarchy to show the world a face while keeping shadows along the walls.

There was another secret. "It's all about the shadow," she'd written. And it was not the shadow from their history, it was their current shadows. How things were covered up, secret under coverings of dishonesty. The Dor monarchy had always been more than just power. It had been about appearances, control, and the deliberate twisting of truth.

"You're saying Elina stumbled upon something?" Ariana pressed. "Something about the Dors?"

"Not exactly. She was interested in the way the Dors manipulated history. How they controlled the narrative. She didn't just study it. She lived it. But." "There was one thing she said, one thing I'll never forget."

Ariana asked, "What was it?"

Sinclair hesitated.

"Elina... she told me that she had learned something about the past. Something about her family, something about her own history," Sinclair added, finally looking at eyes of Ariana. His tone grew more serious. "She told me she wasn't who she was supposed to be. That something was hidden, something that must remain hidden."

Ariana's breath stopped. There it was. the promise of a personal history that Elina had been investigating. A history she might have discovered only to find it was much worse than she had ever dreamed. Something lay hidden in the darkest depths of the Baxter family's history.

Seraphina's voice shattered the silence that had fallen over the room. "So, this conversation, this was the last one she ever had with you?"

Sinclair nodded, his face impossible to read. "Yes. We discussed the ways in which history might repeat itself, the ways in which one might never really be free of the past."

Ariana's eyes sparkled. "And what did you say to her?". "I explained to her that some things, once revealed, are best left alone."

"And you explained this to her at the Royal Tea Party?" Ariana asked. "Yes. I did".

Ariana's thoughts spun, but she remained calm. The discussion had changed, but not as she had anticipated. There were layers to be unraveled. More secrets hidden under the surface of what Elina had discovered. The previous conversation between them was only a teaser. A piece of the greater puzzle that had resulted in her demise.

"I'm interested in the research papers," Ariana said. "What did she hand over to you?". "Papers and notes she had done at Oxford,". "She had written some papers on the Dor period, but there was one that she kept to herself. She gave me a draft just before she died. She said it was a breakthrough. Something nobody else had found out. But she did not want to say any more about it. She said she had to work it up".

Ariana's surprised. A breakthrough? The pieces were finally falling into place, but the puzzle was still far from being solved.

"Do you still have it?" Seraphina demanded.

Sinclair paused before inclining his head. "I do.". This was the first real lead they had, and it was in Elina's work the research, the papers, the final proof of her obsession. The key to discovering what had killed her was in that draft, hidden in Sinclair's office.

"We have to read it," Ariana said.

"Alright then," Sinclair replied, standing up. He pointed toward the door. "Come on."

They followed him along the long corridor.

They were led by Sinclair to a study room in the back of the house, a room that smelled of leather-bound books and dust. The room was lined with massive bookshelves, filled high with books on history, literature, and art. There was a fireplace, grey stones, unused standing in one corner.

Sinclair walked over to his desk and pulled open a drawer. He removed a large folder, its corners frayed from years of wear, and placed it on the desk before them.

"Here it is," he said, his voice now a bit softer.

Ariana's eyes ran over the folder as she opened it slowly, the pages within yellowed with age. They were full of Elina's neat handwriting comments on the Dors, a chart of how they had achieved power, and a draft essay that analyzed the manipulations of the monarchy concerning history. It was one note, however, that caught Ariana's notice.

The message was scribbled in such a hurry as if Elina had been doing it in haste:

"There exists a hidden fact about the family of Baxter's. Dors were not the only one who had authority over shaping the past. My family. We're related. But if I speak, I'll be dead."

A chill ran down the spine of Ariana. Elina had known. She had uncovered something—something evil. And now it was sure: her death had not been an accident. It was only a portion of something much larger.

She closed the folder gently. "It's all here," Ariana said. "We just need to link the dots."

* * * * *

# Chapter 25

# **The Rivalry, the Papers, and the Shadows**

Ariana and Seraphina were still on high alert as Sinclair pulled out a thick pile of papers, ragged at the edges, from his drawer. He set them down on the desk in front of them. There was something in her face. Confusion. But first, there was the issue of Alfanza White, the Duchess of Heirshen, whose name appeared in the background, still echoing from the previous conversation with Sinclair. "You must understand," Sinclair began slowly. "Elina wasn't just an exceptional student . She was the only exceptional student. And that. Well, that created tension. There were people who couldn't stand it." Ariana already sensed it that it would be jealousy, but now it was becoming clearer.

"Alfansa White, Duchess of Heirshen," Sinclair went on, the name on his lips were clear. "Alfansa and Elina hate each other since they were at Oxford. Alfansa, naturally, was a member of an old and illustrious family, and she thought the limelight always right to be hers. Elina, though humble, possessed that gift that some are born with talent for stealing the spotlight without ever having to try. It irritated Alfansa."

Seraphina asked. "What occurred between them? Was it merely academic competition?

Sinclair's smiled. "No, it wasn't just academic rivalry. There was more at stake than that prestige, opportunities, recognition. And it was clear that Elina had the upper hand. I've seen it before. In academic circles, the hunger for recognition can turn friendships into competitions. But with Elina and Alfansa, it was something more. It was a battle for legacy. It became personal. She knew that this was merely the start of what might become a dangerous discovery. "And then?" Ariana asked. "What happened after Oxford?". Sinclair continued, "Well, after graduation, Alfansa went on to become the personal secretary of the Duchess of Heirshen. Elina, on the other hand, found her place in academia, rising through the ranks as a respected historian. But she stayed clear of the aristocracy, away from the set where Alfansa had established herself. The moment of truth, though, arrived when Elina was awarded the esteemed Arthurian History Award. She was the youngest winner in decades. And Alfansa? She couldn't stand it.".

Ariana looked at Seraphina. The puzzle pieces were beginning to fall in place, bit by slow bit. They needed to understand what had happened between these two. It was no longer about academic competition now.

"But why did it get out of hand?" Seraphina asked.

Sinclair's voice heard saying, "Because Elina discovered something that could destroy both of them."

Ariana's heart skipped. "What did she discover?"

He looked into Ariana's eyes. "Something from history that wasn't supposed to be revealed. You see, Elina and Alfansa each had ancestors connected to the Dors.". But whereas Elina was happy to research them, Alfansa had always been obsessed on the notion of being directly descended from the royal line in a very particular manner. Elina's revelation, her study was too close to the actual truth. And that was something neither of them could risk having revealed.

Ariana's heart beat increased. This wasn't a matter of competition anymore. This was power. Legacy. And secrets so unfaithful that one woman had to kill the other before the truth could destroy it all.

"May I?" Ariana asked. Ariana rustled through the pile. Elina's precise handwriting, the mentions of ancient archives, out-of-date books, and the laboriously detailed chronology of the Dor line. And then. There it was. A hasty note scribbled across the foot of a page. Elina's handwriting, unmistakable, urgent, and raw. "Alfansa is hiding something.

Her family's roots go far beyond the Dors. There's another hidden history, one that ties her to the missing heirs. I cannot allow her to learn what I've discovered. It is too risky."

Ariana felt a shiver as she read. Missing heirs? What had Elina discovered that was so incriminating, so scandalous, that it would jeopardize Alfansa's entire reputation?

Seraphina's voice heard asking a question. "Do you believe Elina was murdered to keep this secret?"

Ariana didn't respond at once. It was all falling into clearer perspective now. Elina had discovered something regarding Alfansa's family, something so potent that it had marked her for death. The woman who had excelled academically, who had constructed a life founded on intellectual endeavor, had been destroyed by a truth she was not supposed to discover.

"Perhaps," Ariana whispered. "But there is more to this than simple jealousy or competition. Elina was discovering something much more threatening than a simple academic disagreement."

Sinclair's face grew dark. "You'll have to interview Alfansa personally. She'll never confess anything. But this I can say. She was afraid of what Elina was discovering. Afraid of being revealed."

Ariana's eyes glowed with purpose. "We are going to question her. But we have to know everything that Elina had been researching first. This could be the missing piece we are looking for".

Sinclair nodded solemnly. "Beware. The past has a tendency to catch up with all of us."

As Ariana and Seraphina stood up from the table, the probe had taken a disturbing turn, one that would set them on a trail filled with twists and secrets that would jeopardize the very fabric of history.

* * * * *

# Chapter 26

# The Final Villain

Sinclair rose from the leather sofa, his eyes cold and calculating. He repeated the words slowly, his voice cutting through the tension in the air. "You must try your best to investigate her classmates. Alfansa White cut all ties ages ago, so I recommend focusing on the batch. I have a lot of group photos in the notes. Investigate the people, I have their addresses as well."

Ariana's heart thudded in her chest, the weight of Sinclair's words sinking in. She swallowed hard, her throat dry. She nodded, barely managing to keep her composure, as Seraphina tugged at her wrist and pulled her out of the room. They didn't have time to waste.

Ariana was too focused on Sinclair's instructions to even thank Seraphina as they hurried toward the exit. They were on a mission. She could feel the tightness in her chest, the knot in her stomach growing with every second that passed.

The papers they needed were clutched tightly in Ariana's hands, a bundle of clues—perhaps the key to everything. Outside, the grandeur of the manor loomed before them, bathed in the soft glow of the setting sun. Ariana's breath quickened. Everything felt too quiet, too still, as if the calm before the storm was about to break.

* * * * *

# Chapter 27

# The Malicious Friendship

Ariana was looking at the notes Elina had left. The historian had been nothing less than dedicated in devotion to detail, leaving no rock unturned, no fact unnecessary. It was both her genius and her misery.

Elina had been systematic, documenting every bit of information about Alfansa White's classmates, the individuals who had been around her during those last few days. Elina had been searching for something. Ariana was positive of it. But the deeper she went, the more she could feel that the historian's research had wandered into unfaithful ground. The kind of ground that had killed her. Elina had described at length the classmates, those who were close to Alfansa. And of the names, one stood out from the rest

Cassandra Evelyn Vernbrooke.

The Duchess of Heirshen, a woman who had been seen in the most dazzling society, who had a reputation for grace, style. And yet the report told a different tale.

Elina had likened her to "an problem wrapped in layers of planned behavior." A woman who never lowered her defenses who is perfect but underneath it all, there existed cracks. Slight shades, only distinguished by someone possessing Elina's keen eye.

"Bites her nails when alone, always close to a source of water, nervously washing her hands in public events."

The information in the report seemed familiar. She'd watched the Duchess at hundreds of functions, watched the way she'd pull at the hem of her gown or the way her hands would tremble just before she was to speak. But Ariana had always thought these were the mannerisms of a woman who lived in the public eye, a woman who had to present a flawless image at all times.

But now, those little mannerisms appeared a lot more different. Elina's observations indicated that these were not just habits of nervousness. There was something beneath those movements.

* * * * *

# Chapter 28

# The Duchess of Heirshen

Ariana's eyes came down the page further, reading Elina's notes on the Duchess's physical appearance. Her jaw set as she absorbed the accurate details. "Pale complexion, freckle-like spots around the neck her face always perfectly made up, but under the makeup, the skin under her eyes had the faintest shake, as if she couldn't quite hide her distress."

Ariana's paused. That mark. The same one that Elina had said was "visible but artfully concealed." Ariana had witnessed it at a ball, low on the Duchess's right jawline, a fractured scar that went hidden under her collar. She'd thought it a mishap, perhaps a child's scar, but now looked much more deliberate, like the Duchess had made an effort to conceal it because of something.

But it was the following part of Elina's report that left Ariana gasping.

"The Duchess was involved in a study group some years ago with Alfansa White. They were close friends. Others believe that this closeness allowed for the sharing of personal secrets between the two. Secrets that should not be shared with others.

Ariana reread those lines again and again. Secrets. Elina wrote about the comfortable friendship between the Duchess and Alfansa. As per the report, since the sudden vanishing of Alfansa years ago, the Duchess has been in self-imposed seclusion, fading from public life nearly completely. Ariana's head was spinning now. Could it be? Was this friendship they'd been looking for? Alfansa was back after some time. The answers were there in Ariana's hands, but they were more dangerous than she'd ever imagined.

Elina had penned a description of a particular event, an event that had occurred in the months prior to Alfansa's vanishing. A meeting between the two women, one that nobody had been able to track. "The night before Alfansa disappeared, the Duchess was seen to be more than normally distressed. She asked for a closed meeting with Alfansa a meeting that ended in heated arguments.

Ariana's head reeled. What was it that they might have had a fight over? And why hadn't they ever considered pursuing the link between the Duchess and Alfansa sooner?

But there was something more. Something which brought Ariana to a stop. Elina had written,

"I have cause to suspect that the Duchess of Heirshen is hiding something much more than a mere academic dispute. She might not have been as innocent as everyone has been made to think. Perhaps she was involved in Alfansa's disappearance and reappearance, although the level of her complicity remains unknown."

Ariana carefully placed the report on the floor. The fragments were coming together now. The Duchess, Alfansa, Elina. everything merged around a single point. The truth was so near, and yet Ariana sensed that they were all poised. She had dared to think.

* * * * *

# Chapter 29

# **The Final Decision**

A duchess is very well and good up there. It is almost too dreamlike to believe. It had all been for the sake of the truth, hadn't it? But now, all she could sense was the exhaustion of it. The truth seemed a distant dream.

A feeble voice in her mind said, Drop the case. Life is more than this case. It was not even a thought she could silence anymore. It became louder, more persistent, until she simply could not help but hear it. She would not admit it, but the desire for justice still prevails. But you are the one who profits from it all, she told herself. Money, power, influence. they all ride on you. You can leave. You can just walk away and leave it all behind, and no one will even glance up. You won't have to make any effort.

There was no satisfaction in it, no calm. But what if they say you are a traitor? It would have been difficult for her to turn away, and yet, all this was now sounding distant to her.

She dialed Hannah. It rang once, twice before she ended it. What am I doing? What if I do something stupid? What if it all comes crashing down? She saw the worst possible outcomes: Death. Jail. A lifetime of shame. And then there was a buzz on her phone. Hannah calling.

At last, she picked up her call. You can't let her see this. You can't let anyone see how you are falling apart.

Hannah," she snapped, her voice sharper than she meant it to be, "I dialed by mistake. Any updates on the case?"

There was a pause on the other line, then Hannah's gentle voice heard, "Ariana, everyone is counting on you. This case... It's so confusing. People are losing hope.".

Those words struck her like a slap across the face. Everyone is counting on you.

She needed to do something. She needed to act as if she was still in charge, as if she was still the individual, they all thought she was.

She closed her eyes for an instant, preparing herself. Then, grinding her teeth, she replied, her voice shaking but firm. "I don't know what you're referring to, Hannah," she said a trifle too sharply. "But I'll get to the bottom of it. I always do."

The quietness filled the air after she uttered the words. For a second, she nearly believed she could just say she was fine and go on as if nothing was wrong. Ariana gained confidence despite the voice and aggressively stated "look I know who it is you won't believe me, I hope you are alone in your apartment right now"

Hannah froze and replied "yes who is it Sinclair right"

Ariana interrupted no it is not Sinclair it is a person impossible to control or suspect I think we should stop this case it is. I can't tell you on the phone come to my home fast

Ah-ha! The important revelation is that the Duchess was innocent and Alfansa is the actual killer, not even necessarily the means by which she was killed. Here is a rewritten version keeping that in mind, making the moment one of revelation about the Duchess's innocence and how Alfansa pieces fit into the puzzle

She called her therapist. "Ariana?"

"I need the book," Ariana replied. She couldn't put words to "The one I lent you. It's. significant. I need it now."

There was a silence on the other side. "Ariana, you know."

"I'll bring it back. Please," She requested again, "I just need it."

The phone went quiet for a moment, but Ariana didn't hold out for an answer. She hung up the phone. When she took it down from the shelf. She was seeking answers.

She has gone through the book, which contained snippets of ideas, impressions, hypotheses illegible in quick handwriting across the pages. The case was so complex.

Elina's murder, the Duchess's connection. The leads had always led back to Alfansa, the Duchess's closest friend, but something doesn't seem correct. Ariana's went to a part of the notes that she'd remembered nothing about notes on families, on alliances, on enmities. Her eyes traveled over the names she recognized, the men and women who had been closest to Elina. The ones who had associated with the Duchess. And then her eyes fixated on something a reference to a dialogue. A letter shared between the Duchess and Elina.

Alfansa, the name she'd been noting over for weeks, now stood out. But it wasn't the same. Something had been hidden in the manner in which the letter was phrased. She turned back to the earlier page. There, in a hurried note in the margin of the family trees, was the link she'd overlooked. The Duchess's wedding, the heritage. Alfansa had fought for it, and the letter spoke of a boiling mind. Something Elina had unconsciously awakened when she began to wonder about the fate of the family title. The puzzles were fitting into place.

And the most disturbing aspect was not that Alfansa had motive. It was the fact that she had exploited the Duchess's innocence. The Duchess had been set up as if see is the anti-hero, innocent the entire time. Alfansa had suggested it, seeded the doubt, then poisoned Elina's drink herself. The Duchess had been a pawn in a game she never knew she was playing.

Ariana closed the book. She was on the edge of something that might change everything. The ring of a bicycle stopping outside distracted her. The world outside was just too loud. Ariana went up to the corkboard lined with notes and photos. She began to sweep the board. The notes she had so exactly organized. She tore them off, as if by taking them away, she could strip away the confusion. The discovery concerning Alfansa was too much to leave on the board, out in the open.

Hannah walked in. Her closest friend, observing her in confusion. "Ariana? What's the matter?

Wordlessly, she pushed her phone across the table, revealing Hannah the notes on Elina, the family history, the most important connections. Hannah didn't require explanation. Her eyes dashing faster than Ariana's could follow. Hannah's face changed from confusion to realization. Hannah's started talking. "Wait... Alfansa. She was the one who..."

"She set Duchess up,". "She made everyone believe the Duchess was the killer. But she wasn't". Hannah's couldn't digest the information. "But why? Why would she do that?"

Ariana's held the edges of the book. "Because of the inheritance. The title. The power.". "She used poison. She did it slowly, carefully."

"Cyanide," Ariana told. "It didn't work immediately. She used it in a beverage, to make it appear as though she had an illness, but she didn't. The Duchess. She was her cover. The actual killer is Alfansa."

The investigation was no longer about identifying the killer. It was about how to dismiss the Duchess's name that had bound her to her friend's murder.

But the questions were still there. How far did Alfansa have to go in order to preserve her secret,

and how many individuals assisted her in the process?

Ariana snatched a brown worn notebook in which Elina Sophie Baxter was written and had riddles by Elina. Ready to be released on 8th February and switched on the projector to present the book written by Elina.

* * * * *

# Chapter 30

# The Riddle Notebook

The dim projector came to life. The puzzle pieces coming into place. The words appeared harmless at first reading. Let's figure out the riddles, it will help us in the billions for this case Ariana said to Hannah.

Hannah agreed.

---

Riddle 1:

"In a hall of mirrors, where faces glower,
One truth is hidden under the glare.
A smile, a joke, a word so sharp,
The seed of hatred, almost invisible."

The seed of hatred. This wasn't about a mere conflict. It was more. The reflections of who they were covering their true emotions. And the root was a single word, intense.

The term called to attention Elina's sharp, hurtful words at Oxford, the sort of which they spoke about unnoticeably in doorways. Alfansa... She spoke harsh things in private, intended for her and for Elina, and for possibly. to the duchess regarding Elina.

And there it was. Alfansa had instilled the seed of hate, but Cassandra... Cassandra who was a classmate to both Elina and Alfansa and later went on to become Duchess after marriage had cultivated it into something so much darker.

---

Riddle 2: The Price of Revenge

In the second riddle, every word a painful urging toward the truth.

"An insult lies deep beneath the skin,
Where vengeance resides, and darkness starts.".
The tongue that lashes with cruel power,
Will taste revenge in the dead of night.

Ariana did not have to think twice. She already knew.

An insult cuts very close to the bone. It had always been more than just an insult. It had been thoughtful. Planned. Abrupt and merciless and venomous. But no one had realized quite how much they had wounded Elina, how they had driven her to the edge. And that was when it was sudden. Elina never forgave Alfansa. She had spent years planning her revenge, secretly watching her. And when the time was right, Elina wanted to give punishment.

Ariana's could remember the spark in Elina's eyes when she had talked of Alfansa. _

---

Riddle 3: Oxford's Darkest Secret

"In halls where scholars have their say,
The most intellectual minds the truth do seek.
But there exists a shadow within the light,
Where two are tied by their shared power."

Ariana's mind jumped instantly to Oxford. It was where they had raised their brains. She was certain that the Duchess and Elina had met there. But what had united them?

"The brightest minds". That was certain. The Duchess, born Cassandra Vernbrooke, had been an aristocrat, powerful and privileged. Elina, brilliant, had equaled that power with her mind. Both had occupied the top of society.

The secret was the phrase mutual might. They weren't merely in Oxford together. They had discovered power in one another or maybe it was the power that they possessed over their enemies. The mutual might was a game of dominance, over knowledge over Alfansa.

---

Riddle 4: The Tea Party's Poison

Ariana's proceeded to the next riddle. She knew this was on its way.

"Drops in a cup, so accurate,
A show of generosity, yet icy to the touch.

A sip, a smile, and the game's end,
A drink that hints, closing the name."

Ariana able to see fragments fit together. Three drops of cyanide. She remembered it from before. The tea party where Elina was the honored guest, just prior to her death.

Her mind went back and she saw the hostess a fragile smile on her face as she poured the tea Then the duchess had been the one to take the first sip. The game's end.

Now it got seriously creepy Elina foresaw her own death .... Ariana thought confused.

Ariana's could come to conclusion that Alfansa was the person whose hand served tea to Elina. The tea which had poison. The act of niceness was merely an echo of the cruel revenge to come.

---

Riddle 5: The Last Riddle

The last riddle. the last of the series was the most difficult, the one that would tie everything together.

"In silence, she stands as a guest of grace,
Her breath in the air, but no trace to face.
The final drop falls, unseen, unheard,
The end of the line, as the silence stirred."

No evidence. The last drop the most important one was designed to be undetectable. The poison had already taken effect before the duchess had sipped the final draught.

Ariana's hands shook as she put it together. Three drops. Each one a move in a deadly way.

And Alfansa's ultimate revenge.

The silence woke up. It was not the guests or the hosts or the crowd that had created the uproar. It was Elina.

* * * * *

# Chapter 31

# The Transmission of Codes

As Ariana gazed at the riddles before her, the reality was now evident. Alfansa, the woman she had previously thought to be the mastermind behind their destruction.

Elina was only a pawn in an infinitely greater game, Alfansa's game. The cruel words that passed between them, the poison in the tea, the silent revenge. All these pointed to one thing. Alfansa had known the Duchess for years. She had observed her weakness and threatening to expose it. She manipulated it. She had watched her.

And when the moment had arrived, Alfansa had dispensed the setback. Hard. Mercilessly. She was alone now with this knowledge. Merciless mind that had constructed this elaborate scheme of lies and revenge. But of one thing Alfansa was sure. She had won. Now, with these riddles, Ariana would have to do the cleanup.

Ariana remained before the projector, running through the clues, the riddles, the fragments of the puzzle that had appeared so all over the map before. Now, they all fit.

Ariana's voice came swiftly. "Hannah, it's Alfansa. She was the one behind it all. She murdered Elina."

Hannah blinked in confusion. "Wait, is it Alfansa? But. the Duchess Cassandra she was Elina's opponent, not Alfansa! The Duchess was the one who disliked her. Ariana said in firm voice, "The Duchess didn't kill Elina. Alfansa did. She disliked Elina just as much as Cassandra did. But Alfansa was much more careful.". "But why? Alfansa and Duchess were best friends. Why would Alfansa want her best friend in prison. ". Ariana looked directly at Hannah. "That's the thing you're not seeing. Alfansa didn't care about being friends. She wanted the spotlight. And once Cassandra married into the royals, once she had the attention of the court and society, Alfansa was pushed aside. She hated Elina, but even more she hated the way the Duchess had everything she'd always wanted fame, power and respect."

Ariana's continued. "Cassandra married into the royal family to be in the limelight. She wanted to be loved, respected. She craved attention. But she couldn't bear the fact that Elina, the historian, the woman of knowledge was always the one everyone looked up to. The Duchess couldn't tolerate that. She needed Elina out of the way.". But she couldn't do it herself. She didn't want to kill Elina. Hannah's eyes widened. "And Alfansa wanted that". "Yes. Alfansa manipulated the Duchess's jealousy. She knew the Duchess hated Elina, so she made Elina appear to be a threat to the duchess.". She used that jealousy, that fear of being overshadowed, to play on her and make her think that Elina was the true enemy. She made Cassandra believe that Elina was dangerous that Elina's influence would ultimately overshadow hers even among the royal family. So, what did Alfansa do? She poisoned Cassandra's mind against Elina, making her to think that the only way to protect herself was to eliminate Elina. She used Elina's long written riddle which was a part of college game earlier in Oxford and doesn't mean any harm to anyone. She made Duchess believe that this riddle is the Elina's plan to kill Duchess. Hannah asked, "So it wasn't about simply killing Elina. It was about getting the Duchess to think that Elina was her enemy."

"Exactly," Ariana said. "But it was more than that. Alfansa didn't just want Elina out of the way.". She wanted to step in, take all that Elina possessed. She wanted the power, attention, spotlight, which Elina dominated. And she knew only through getting into the Duchess's ear, turning her mind around, and leading her to believe that she must assassinate Elina could she achieve this. But she didn't approach it directly. She operated behind the scenes.

Ariana gestured towards the screen, where Elina's notebook riddles were still visible. "Those riddles? They weren't games. They were clues. A game Alfansa played with the Duchess's mind. They were her means of making the Duchess doubt Elina further, making her the enemy, while Alfansa stayed behind.". She ensured the riddles were suspicious enough to make Cassandra think that Elina was evil, that she had to be stopped before she destroyed everything.

Hannah's face turned dark. "But why did no one suspect it? Why didn't the Duchess realize it?

"Because Cassandra was blinded by jealousy," Ariana replied softly but firmly. "Alfansa knew just how to fuel that jealousy, just how to manipulate it in order to control her. And when the tea party arrived, the ideal time to frame the duchess for crime, Alfansa ensured the poison was in Elina's cup. Three drops of cyanide, just enough to kill her without it being obvious. She was being attacked directly Cassandra never had a clue."

Hannah took a step back, the truth breaking on her face. "So, Alfansa set Elina up, played the Duchess into thinking she was the enemy. And now, Elina's dead."

Ariana nodded gravely. "Exactly. And Alfansa? She gets away with everything she desires, the attention, the power, the limelight. The only thing left is to ensure that she pays the price."

Hannah blinked. "But. how do we prove it?"

Ariana gazed at the screen again. "We'll reveal everyone the truth. We have the riddles, the manipulation, the poison. Now, all we need to do is tie the dots. And when we do, Alfansa won't be able to cover up."

What we have is records about Elina and her reports and we need to let Duchess know the truth.

We can get Alfansa's fingerprint as she was secretary for Duchess and all maids finger prints will be with Duchess. Let us verify and prove.

* * * * *

# Chapter 32

# **The Crucial Investigation**

The group met in the dark conference room. Maya, Benedict, Seraphina, and Sebastian sat at the table. Ariana stood at the front, having a pile of papers. Hannah stood at her side.

Ariana spoke to the group. "We have collected enough evidence to obtain a warrant for Alfansa's arrest. The manipulation, the poisoning, the riddles which Elina wrote in Oxford and which riddles Alfansa used to show Duchess how evil Elina trying to eliminate her. To make Duchess believe that Elina was poisonous but in truth it was not. It all links to her."

Hannah agreed. "We must speak with Cassandra. She must know the way she was manipulated."

Ariana switched to Maya. "Benedict, Seraphina, Sebastian. Set the warrant. Hannah, and Maya let's visit the Duchess. It is time she realized and you're coming with me"

Ariana exited from the study room and went quickly to her room and she opened up her well-chosen and designed closet dressed in a straight black denim and a crisp white top with a plain grey one button coat and went over confidently to the palace. She glanced at her black watch it was 6 PM the doors close at 7:30 if we leave now, we can get in at 6 :10 to the max she told herself the elevators slid open with a soft ping she stepped inside always checking on the time and in an instant all of them got into the car. she checked the evidence again. Ariana scrolled through her phone. They all were in royal mansion. Ariana walked toward the Duchess's private quarters. The guards moved aside knowing the detectives. Inside, Cassandra sat beside the window, staring out at the extensive gardens. She turned when they came in.

"Detectives," she said, her voice firm. "To what do I owe this visit?"

Hannah moved forward, her voice assertive but kind. "Your Grace, we have found evidence that indicates you were manipulated into thinking that Elina was a threat.". "Manipulated? By whom? I told you Elina was always the innocent one".

Maya set a folder on the table in front of them. "By Alfansa. She manipulated your jealousy and insecurities to make you turn on Elina."

Ariana with sorry face started conversation. "Your grace she means your best friend Alfansa is not who you believe she is. she was fond of you before you married the royals but then came to regret your limelight. ". She gently completed

Hannah went on, "The riddles, the indirect suggestions, those were all part of her scheme to make you distrust Elina, to make you think she was conspiring against you."

Cassandra's face went white as the truth dropped in. "No. I. I was so blinded by my own fears, my own insecurities. I couldn't see it."

Your grace we have missing evidence and it is Alfansa's fingerprint could you give us the fingerprint of all your maids.

Yes, indeed she said with a soft voice

The duchess pointed to the cupboard that radiated in the fresh and elegant moonlight with golden stitching she received a white chart that had smudged black impressions of a hand.

Ariana received the chart in her hand after curtsying to the duchess. Ariana took a small carry-on sanitizer shaped machine and took the ornamental dagger and displayed it. The duchess remarked that is a Heirshen family heirloom dagger how is it with you.

Maya explained Alfansa employed it to stab Luna your grace the Duchess nodded while she appeared to be crying inside.

Maya continued, "Alfansa knew how to manipulate your emotions. She knew you felt threatened by Elina's brains and power. She nurtured those feelings, until you thought Elina was your enemy."

Ariana cut in "She means Alfansa blinded you way too much she felt you where her pawn is the sum up" she concluded using the same tone

Hannah concluded saying. "You were a victim, just like Elina. Alfansa manipulated you in order to take out her competitor. Your grace".

Cassandra's eyes welled with tears. "I. I didn't think she has gone so far. I was trying to protect myself, my position. But I was nothing more than a pawn in her game."

Hannah nodded. "It's not too late to set things right. We can reveal the truth, justify your name, and get Alfansa in prison."

Cassandra rose from chair. "Then let's go. For Elina. For the truth."

Ariana specifically mentioned her intention is to send you to jail for Elina's murder which is her chance to get the limelight as noble. Read these documents when you are finished call us if you need anything. She stepped out scrolling her phone for warrant information.

There was a scanned document sent by Seraphina the warrant she shrilly added. We go to the maid house residences on the other side of town. Maya stepped out I will go assist Seraphina I will give you the warrant.

* * * * *

# Chapter 33

# The Arrest

Back in the grace room, Maya handed over the signed warrant to Ariana. "It's official. We can search Alfansa's house and arrest her." Ariana nodded. "Let's take her in."

Alfansa was sitting in the maid's drawing room, a tea glass in her hand, not knowing what was about to meet her. The doorbell rang. She got up to answer it, smiling.

She opened the door to find herself face to face with Ariana, Hannah, Maya, Benedict, Seraphina, and Sebastian. "Alfansa", Ariana started, "you're under arrest for murder and manipulation of the Duchess."

Alfansa's eyes swelled. "What? That's ridiculous!"

Hannah pushed forward, displaying the folder full of evidence. "We have evidence of your participation. The riddles, the poison, the manipulation. Everything was engineered by you."

Alfansa's voice was cold. "You don't know what you're saying. I did what I had to do to live."

Maya said, "You manipulated the Duchess's weaknesses to make her hate Elina. You contaminated her mind, as you spoiled Elina."

Seraphina took a step forward. "And now, you'll pay."

Alfansa's disobedience crumbled as she was hand cuffed by Dorian vale. "I did not mean to go this far. I merely wished to be acknowledged, to be noticed."

"Dorian halted, as she screamed, forcing her to sit down with handcuffs bound.

Is it Alfansa? because this is not your first killing Alfansa, if I am correct your 50th killing and 51st killing is Luna as she got close to reality. You are psychopathic. For the limelight and attention, you killed family members, friends and fellow colleagues all so only you are the spotlight. Detectives never discovered". but I probe deeper than the rest, Alfansa for your offense, you will be placed in maximum security prison or executed but I suggest maximum security prison to the police, I have all your information. Your fingerprints are matching. You even stole Heirshen royal's family treasures. You ought to be punished. "Your ambition resulted in murder. Now, you will pay the price."

As Alfansa was escorted away, the team looked at each other in relief and determination. The case was closed.

Ariana experienced the chill breeze of London and her happiness was certain, but then a voice so familiar was heard "No stop my friend"

It was a female with olive complexion and a beautiful voice

It was Ella the butler who was spy.

Ariana grinned and said in a sly tone "Ella how many did you kill, more or less, either way prison for you"

Ella replied "I was the real companion. Her only best friend. I assisted her with details from every house. So please take me to jail as well" Ella pleaded.

"It is waiting for you anyway Ella medium security prison for a lifetime" Hannah concluded

* * * *

# Chapter 34

# The Relaxing Sip

Ariana awoke to the bright sun. She rose from her bed and clicked off her alarm and she headed to the bathroom to brush her teeth in quiet after what seemed like an eternity. She dressed in a loose shirt and black comfortable pants. A soothing atmosphere which never existed yesterday.

She walked through the fresh beauty of glass windows and quiet empty space the dining hall was filled with the aroma of heavenly bread and butter and Nutella spread bread combined with a hint of cold coffee was just perfect. She sat on the first seat munching the bread which she normally found plain to be just perfect. She carried the coffee in the shiny surface glossy in the light. The black deep frame provided stark contrast with the vivid red trimmings, commanding the space with authority. Within, the glass organizers were a flawless show of precision. Tidy rows of writing supplies lined the first row. Smooth pens and markers in every color of the rainbow. The pens were coded by color, soft pastels to deep rich tones, each categorized for its use. Red pens for important details, black for accuracy. Markers, wide and fine, lined up beside one another, shining with eagerness.

Then rows of journals and notebooks graced the shelves. Some in worn leather bindings, others sleek but functional. They all held Ariana's secrets, plans, and ideas, with some pages having scrawled writings in rush, others neat and systematic, all indicative of her organized chaos. Behind them were glass containers full of bright tubes of paint. reds, blues, and whites. Next to them were brushes, their delicate bristles pointed, waiting to bring Ariana's ideas to life.

The bottom drawers held color coded boxes of threads. Silk, cotton, and linen, each spool marked with an alphanumeric code known only to Ariana. Elevator staring upwards towards the clear tranquil sky with white clouds she thought of Elina and Luna then proceeded to her favorite giant red and black cupboard she pulled out a book that was filled with simple colorless images of her house she also picked up a pack of colors and headed towards her table a plain marble table and a cup of her coffee. She sat and got her phone and scheduled an appointment with her therapist next day. She experienced calm in every drop.

* * * * *

THE END

www.ingramcontent.com/pod-product-compliance
Lightning Source LLC
Chambersburg PA
CBHW021531150726
47990CB00006B/2184